DEATH'S DEMISE

DEATHLY ENCOUNTERS BOOK THREE

DEATH'S DEMISE

DEATHLY ENCOUNTERS BOOK THREE

CRYMSYN HART

SEVENTH STAR PRESS

Cover art and design: Enggar Adirasa
Cover art in this book copyright © 2017 Enggar Adirasa & Seventh Star
Press, LLC.

Editor: Scott Sandridge

Published by Seventh Star Press, LLC.

ISBN Number: 978-1-948042-00-0

Seventh Star Press
www.seventhstarpress.com
info@seventhstarpress.com

Publisher's Note:
Death's Demise is a work of fiction. All names, characters, and places are
the product of the author's imagination, used in fictitious manner. Any
resemblances to actual persons, places, locales, events, etc. are purely
coincidental.

Printed in the United States of America

First Edition

BOOK THREE

CHAPTER ONE

I stood in the solace of the graveyard, taking in the quiet of the world around me. The spirits who lingered in this forgotten place knew better than to interrupt me. The moon hung low. Opposite the pale orb, the pastels of dawn dimmed the stars. As the world shifted from darkness to dawn, life froze. I reached out with all my senses, taking in the beauty and harmony of the moment. Only for a few precious minutes none of the burdens of my existence hung on me in this treasurable time.

The calmness within the boneyard renewed my spirit. Of late my nerves had been bristling. Existence seemed gritty, covered in a fine sand I couldn't brush off. A breeze rattled the leaves from the boughs. They drifted to the forest floor below, adding to the growing mounds of reds, oranges, and yellows. When I was a kid, I'd jump in the large piles my father would rake before he burned them. Now they gathered around the slate stones and tree trunks. Instead of bringing me peace, it added to the growing unease settling on my shoulders.

Something wasn't right in the universe.

I couldn't put my finger on it no matter the avenue I pursued. My psychic senses foretold nothing. I no longer felt the pull to collect souls. Don't get me wrong, I enjoyed being a grim reaper, but I also missed being human. I took a calming breath. The past was in the past. Although I could tamper with time and fix my grievous errors, I didn't mess with it no matter what the temptation.

"But there's always temptation. It's a basic human necessity."

Damnit. The stench of sulfur permeated the air. Lucifer, The Devil, or Mastema as he was known to all the angels, enjoyed crashing in at the most inopportune moments. "What do you want?" Dawn crested, spreading its brilliance over the boneyard.

His fingers trailed down the side of my cheek. The caresses felt real enough that I could've sworn he was beside me. However, no one was there. The wispy reminders of souls who lingered in the cemetery retreated because of his presence. It didn't matter where I went, he would find me, again and again. He had almost entered into our world to spread his evil to all of humanity. All dimensions were closed off to him once more, and he was locked away in Hell. No matter how tight the doorways were sealed, some places remained thin. This was one of those, at least for me, where the veil could be breached. What else was a graveyard for a grim reaper but a portal into purgatory and the world of the dead?

"You know what I want. Take me up on my offer and let me pleasure you one of these days. Kerstin, you may not realize it, but you stand much my equal. It'd only take a little bit to elevate you to stand by my side for all time."

A tremor of desire ran down my spine at the thought of ever seeing him again. Many believed the Devil had horns. In the guise I saw, he was the most ravishing creature I had ever laid my eyes on. He was lust personified. "You already know my answer, Mastema. I'll never allow you into this world. You may have gotten my blood and my death to open the doorway before, but you never claimed my soul."

"It isn't your soul that I'm after, Kerstin, merely your friendship. Even if you don't wish to acknowledge it, I owe you a boon."

"I'm not one of your devoted followers who blindly renounced their souls to gain some stripped down version of the power you supposedly offer. I have no need for such abilities or promises."

He chuckled so softly longing rolled through my body. Damn. Even his very laugh turned me on and made me question my own sanity.

"I'm the Prince of Darkness. I invented every base yearning and debauchery you can imagine that lives within the human psyche. I have no need for your soul now. Our last meeting was something to cherish. I had no knowledge you were a grim reaper. The power of your soul would have added to the power to let me escape. All the other spirits who were pulled through my rift made a wonderful addition to hell. You really should see it sometime. You might find it more to your liking than that eternal purgatory you linger in."

"Enough taunting, Lucifer. Leave me be. I'm not going to give in, and your incessant prattling is enough to drive me mad. I won't turn from my course and slip into hell. I'm a reaper first and foremost."

"Maybe you are, and maybe you're not. Either way just remember that you're the one who set events in motion."

I rolled my eyes. I was still cleaning up my mess from my last lifetime as a grim reaper when I got Sariel trapped in Death's Dance. The settlement had been a thriving frontier town formed by murderers, thieves, and every low life scum imaginable. Over time that lawlessness spread and innocent people were getting hurt. The women of the town were tired of all the violence and called upon one of their own to do something about it. The witch called down a curse upon the town. In my former incarnation as Lissandra, I had heard her call for death and went to her. Than and Sariel had followed. Because of my decision to collect the souls, we had been wrapped into the web of the plague the woman wrought upon the town. A giant tornado decimated Death's Dance. Than and I escaped the blight, leaving Sariel behind. Because of that, ramifications rippled throughout the universe.

One such consequence was Death's Dance had become something like the Bermuda Triangle and Gettysburg wrapped into one. It was an otherworldly beacon that could not be switched off. It was in this place that the Devil's serial killer had brought me back, hoping to take my soul and use it as the final key to open the gateway to Hell.

"Yeah. Yeah. Tell me something I don't know. Now go away."

Mastema didn't answer. He had withdrawn from this world. Instead, I was left all alone with the spirits who slowly returned to their graves. As the sun rose higher, the coming day didn't bolster my mood. I couldn't shake the feeling that something was skewed in the universe or at least in this dimension. I stared at the ribbons of yellow woven through the blue horizon. Than was off doing his reaper duties. Soon he would come home to me. That would put me at ease for a while. Until he returned, something picked at my consciousness. When I gazed into the future along the branches of possibilities, all I ended up with were dead ends.

There were no answers.

Whatever was coming would have to unfold, and I was going to bear witness to it.

CHAPTER TWO

"**A**ren't you supposed to be writing?"

I raked my fingers through my hair before glancing away from the monitor screen and the blinking cursor that had become my curse of late. Than stood in the doorway. His blond hair hung loose about his shoulders. His pale skin could have marked him for a vampire. Those intense blue-gray eyes of his could break the lock on my soul and stare into its depths. He had found the house I lived in and rewrote a few strands of time to inform the world I'd never been taken out of it. The first time I had seen him in my dreams was in one of two places: the cemetery we brought souls to and the great oak hanging tree in Death's Dance. They were powerful gateways between the worlds. But now I didn't have to dream about him. He was with me always. A token of his love hung around my neck, a feather plucked from his own wing.

I rolled my eyes before flipping him off. "I'm not in the mood."

"Your deadline's coming up. Weren't you supposed to be writing a sequel to your break out fictional novel? The great

Kerstin Palmer, psychic extraordinaire, author, television personality, and grim reaper…shall I go on?" Than walked in and pushed my chair back into the wall. He placed his arms on the chair, trapping me within it. The shreds of his black cloak cut into my flesh. I didn't flinch at the pain. I had felt worse.

"I'll make the deadline. I'm just having a troublesome day." I kissed him lightly. Another coil from his cloak slipped around my neck. It tightened seeking to squelch the life within me. "Can you get your cloak under control?"

"It's just happy to see you. Can't blame it for being eager, can I?" he chuckled.

"No. I guess not. I hate it when you're gone, but it does get me to focus on my writing or appointments. If you were around all the time, then nothing would get done. You are such a wonderful distraction." The threads constricted around my neck and burned. I closed my eyes and let my robes encase me. His uttered a small squeal and pulled away.

"You're no fun."

I poked him in the ribs. "I thought you said I had a deadline to meet."

Than sat back on the desk and crossed his arms. His grim reaper attire faded away to reveal jeans and a black T-shirt. I released mine to the shadows leaving me in the pajama pants and tank top I had on. He traced my neck where his cloak touched me. His cool flesh made the burns feel better, but they'd soon heal. In my current situation, I healed pretty fast.

"I thought you said you were having a troubling day. Did something happen with collecting a soul? Some dark spirit attack you? Only the stupid ones try that with a reaper."

"It wasn't one of the stupid ones. It was the Prince of Darkness attempting to entice me again." Than's eyes flashed with anger. His bony grimace appeared for a moment. "Don't worry. I told him to go back to hell."

"Did he go?"

"He wasn't completely within this realm, just talking to me, making me feel the slight brush of his hand. Nothing more."

"He has no power over you. He can't enter this world, and we *don't* go into his. You know that. The stars must align again for that, and I'm not willing for you to be used for bait."

"I know. I know. I needed some peace and quiet to fill the noise in my mind. Plus, I've sensed that something is off. He wants me to fulfill the boon he owes me."

"Are you?" Than asked.

"Of course not. He wasn't the reason why I went to find some peace and quiet. I was watching the sunrise to feel the tranquility, but I got the impression the universe is unbalanced. Can't you feel it?"

Than face knotted in concentration. The wind chime by the window tinkled its haunting melody. Underneath it I saw a little girl with brown pigtails in a knee length pale blue dress. Deep purple bruises created circles underneath her brown eyes.. She was ghastly pale. Deep purple bruises created circles underneath her deep brown eyes. Blood spattered the front of her dress, and a large gash serrated her throat. Her feet were bare and several raw scrapes showed on her knees. A blue ribbon dangled from one of her pigtails. She wiggled her fingers underneath the wind chime, and it moved once more. An echo of her girlish laughter flitted through the office and curled my bones.

"I don't feel anything." Than looked in the direction of the child. "What are you looking at?"

I gestured at the little girl. "Her? She's right there."

"Kerstin, there's nothing there. Are you sure you're feeling okay?" His eyes were shadowed with worry. "Maybe your encounter today shook you up more than you know."

I summoned all my strength and hit his shoulder. He rubbed the spot and frowned. How could he not see her when I did? "I'm not crazy, and it has nothing to do with Mastema. Something *is* going on."

"I'm sure you'll figure it out. I'm going to get some dinner. How about Greek food?"

I kept my gaze locked on the little girl who was now skipping around the perimeter of my room. Her pigtails bounced and her blue ribbon bobbed. "Greek's fine."

"I'll be back."

The absence of his presence filled the room. The soul did another lap around the room as I came out from behind my desk. Right before she got to me, she disappeared. Her laugh came from my desk. I peered underneath it. Something yanked my hair. I spun around to try and see the little devil. "Not funny, little girl. Come on out."

A cold breeze brushed against my cheek. I grabbed at the draft, hoping to snare her, but my hand passed through thin air. Something hit the back of my legs. The chair spun behind me and my visitor peered out from behind it. She dashed toward the door. This time I caught her arm. Her cold look and the pout told me she wasn't happy about being captured, but I wasn't in the mood. She struggled to break my grasp, but no phantom could escape death's grip no matter how hard they tried. I clutched her shoulders and looked her in the eye. "What do you want?"

"Leave me alone!" she shouted with a raspy, hollow sound.

"How can I leave you alone when you came here looking for me? You know what I am because I can touch you. I'm not going to hurt you. Tell me what you want."

The lost girl twirled her finger around her left pigtail. The distrust in her eyes made me wonder what she had been through. Her bottom lip quivered. "Don't you want to play with me?"

Not really. I wasn't about to let her go in case she vanished and I couldn't find her again. "I'll play with you once you tell me what happened to you, and I'll even give you a cookie. How does that sound?" Every little kid loved sweets, and because I lived in both worlds I could make it so she could actually eat the food.

"Cookie first." Her lips turned up in a triumphant smile.

"Fine, but stay here." I rushed into the kitchen and grabbed a couple of peanut butter oatmeal chocolate chip cookies and hoped they would suffice. She dug into them as though she hadn't eaten in forever. Once she wiped the crumbs from her mouth, her eyes held more trust. "Are you ready to talk to me now?"

She nodded and smiled. The gesture emphasized the gaping gash along her throat. A small trail of blood dribbled down her neck and onto her dress. A few pieces of cookie followed. A wave of nausea came over me. The deep wound leaked a little bit more as she laughed and twirled around the room. The chimes tingled from her movement. The pages on my desk from my latest manuscript lifted from their stack. Something remained off about her. I wasn't sure if it was how she had appeared, or because only I could see her. The way she asked for the cookies was too giddy and too creepy even for me. Something so innocent shouldn't have something so horrible happen to them.

"Are you going to tell me why you're here?" I leaned against my desk. She giggled and the wind chimes sounded again. A small breeze danced around me, and she swirled by in a blur of white. I crossed my arms over my chest. I didn't spend much time around children. Once she calmed down, my visitor stared at me with those big brown eyes. Her gaze made me feel tiny and grated on me the wrong way.

"You're no fun." She pouted.

"Of course, I'm no fun. I'm a grown up." I smiled, but she didn't seem amused by the comment.

"Aren't you going to play with me?"

"I will. We agreed I'd give you a cookie, and then you'd tell me why you're here. Why are you here?"

The strangeness I experienced about the child reared again like a ferocious beast. I gritted my teeth against it. Whatever this strangeness, it wasn't her fault. She had been alone for quite some time and somehow, she found me. What disturbed me the most was that Than couldn't see her. Being a reaper, he should've been able to see any spirit.

"*Fine*. You're so much nicer than the other one was. He was mean to me."

"You said that before. What other one?"

"You know…the one like you."

"What do you mean the one like me?"

"The one who looks like a skeleton dressed in black robes. He found me in my home. I was waiting for Mommy and Daddy to come back. They never did. He said he could take me to a better place…" Her eyes brimmed with tears and twisted my heart. She drew in a labored breath, sucking in the air through the hole in her throat. It sounded like another reaper had found her at the scene of her family's murder. Or maybe it was some abandoned house. I wasn't going to ask about the gruesome details of her death. She might not even remember or even realize she was dead. Sometimes they waited for their loved ones, trapped in a hell of their own making. Even I, who had control of the dead, did not have *absolute* control. Sometimes they didn't aspire to crossover to the other side, and I wouldn't force them.

"What happened to the other reaper who helped you?"

Two large tears rolled down her cheek. Her lower lip quivered. Maybe it was overkill. Maybe she was a better actress then I gave her credit for. Maybe it wasn't an act and something gruesome had happened to her. The whole idea of it rolled within my mind. After becoming human again, I'd become too skeptical. I waited for her to spout off she was a minion sent by the devil to woo me over to his side. I shook my head at the idea. *This is a hurt child who needs my help.*

"He led me from the house into the woods. As we walked, the trees turned into tombstones. They were all overgrown. It scared me. Shadows moved between the gravestones. He squeezed my hand and led me to this great wall of fog. If I went through the curtain of mist, he said, I could see my parents again. I let go of his hand and started to go. A cold wind came up. The sky grew black. I heard a howl in the distance. Thunder cracked all around us. He told me to get behind him and had a long stick in his hand. He swung it at something. There was a lot of noise. I ran and hid behind a big marker. I peeked out and saw these enormous dogs. He screamed. I covered my ears from the noise. I shut my eyes and hoped it would all stop. I waited, and they didn't come after me. The sky went back to normal. I ran back in the forest again."

The hairs stood up on the back of my neck knowing her reaper had been attacked. Only certain things could kill a reaper. One such weapon was our scythes. The other was a sickle which the serial killer brandished when he came after me last year. How he had gotten it, I still didn't know. It sounded as though some kind of animal assaulted the other reaper. If her story was true, which I tended to think it was, someone had to be told. Someone should've noticed reapers going missing. Azrael would've said something because he was the boss. Since I hadn't heard anything, it concerned me more.

"Okay, something happened to him. How did you find me?"

She twirled her fingers around her braid and chewed on her lip. "I-I just felt you. I don't know how to explain it. I kept on walking, and then I had this tug here." She gestured to her heart. "I've been watching you for a couple of days. You seemed nice. Then you were talking to that scary man. I didn't want to come when he was here ..." the rest of her words rolled into sobs and hiccups.

I drew her into my arms and rubbed her back lightly to comfort her. It didn't surprise me she witnessed Mastema talking to me. *Maybe she's part of his grand design. Play on my sympathies and snare me. I wouldn't put it past him. He's the devil after all. She seems genuine.* But that was the thing. The devil wrapped in an innocent guise manipulating me. Maybe he found a way back into this world without me knowing. I bit my cheek and pushed aside my doubts. *No, she has to be telling the truth.*

Something terrible was coming.

"It's okay." I forced a smile. "Don't worry. Nothing's going to harm you while you're with me. The man you saw the other day, what did he look like?"

She wiped her eyes. "I don't really know. He was a shadow with huge wings. It was kinda like he was there, and then he wasn't there. I was frightened of him. That was why I hid."

"You don't have anything to be afraid of with him. He's... well it's complicated, but he won't hurt you. He can't come into this world unless... something else happens. Now tell me your name."

"It's Morana."

"That's a pretty name for a pretty girl. I'm Kerstin. Would you be willing to go back to the graveyard with me?" I needed to see if anything remained of the reaper or if any clues were left behind by the animals she described.

"Do I have to?" The trepidation in her eyes sparked my concern, but I wouldn't let anything happen to her. I had a duty to discover what attacked this reaper. They were my brethren. If this beast was left unchecked, it would eventually come after me and Than as well. Nothing could happen to the man I loved. I nearly lost him once, and I wasn't about to let it happen again.

"I'm not going to force you, but I'd appreciate it if you did. There are more cookies in it for you if you do."

Her eyes brightened at the mention of more sweets. "And some milk to go with them. I'm also really hungry. Do you have any food?"

"After we get back. How does that sound?"

She nodded.

"You're brave doing this."

"I know."

I held out my hand and she twined her fingers through mine. The coldness of death slipped through my veins when she touched my flesh. I left behind the warmth of humanity. The weight of my wings brought familiar comfort. I trailed my fingers over the feather pendant Than had given me. It leant me some strength and courage. If I unearthed something, I would go directly to Azrael.

CHAPTER THREE

The dimensions parted once we walked over the threshold of my office door. Mist captured us and parted to reveal endless rows of gravestones. Various kinds from all different ages along with crypts and mausoleums housed the dead. Trees were peppered here and there. At the very end, a thick drape of gray haze shot out vapor tendrils that caressed the graves like long forgotten lovers.

Morana clenched my hand as we walked down a row. Her fear was palpable, like a second heartbeat that throbbed against my skin. I took in my surroundings. The grass on the plots never grew too tall to obscure the stones. Each marker told a story of the soul who had walked this very same path. Snakes of fog slithered along the paved path. One touched my black cloak and shrunk back.

"How do you do that?" Morana asked.

"What do you mean?"

"You look scary now like the other one did."

I ran my fingers down my cheek. I didn't have to look in a mirror to know my face was a death's head. The illusion fell away and the distress left her eyes. "Better?" I poked her nose.

She giggled.

"It happens when I switch to being a reaper. I don't even notice it anymore. Remember behind every skull there's a person, or at least another angel."

Her eyes lit up even more. "You're an angel." The awe in her tone made me smile. "I didn't know that."

"Yup. We don't all have white fluffy wings or sit on clouds and play harps."

"Do you have a halo?"

Halos. I didn't think I had one. Maybe there was one hanging over me. I passed my hand over the top of my head. "Nope. Guess they forgot to give me one. Or maybe I'm not that kind of angel. I think I'm cooler."

"I agree."

"Where did the other reaper take you? Can you bring me there?"

Morana slipped away from me and turned, taking in the lay of the land. She chose one of the paths between the stones. I followed behind her as she led the way. Something shimmered on the horizon. A large pond surrounded by weeping willows lay before us. Their wispy branches sagged across the surface of the water. The grass was wilder than what I had seen. This place had an older feeling to it than the boneyard I was used to. Slate stones marked the graves instead of marble. The trees were thicker around, and the roads between the markers broken up in some spots.

"Over there." Morana pointed to a knoll on the other side of the pool.

I started toward the hill when I noticed she wasn't behind me. "Are you coming?"

She shook her head no.

"There's nothing to fear."

"I don't want to."

She had come this far without balking. I bit my tongue from the harsh words that threatened to spill from my lips. "Okay, but wait here for me."

Morana plopped down and plucked the long strands of grass. The ground was soft as I climbed the mound. The view from the top showed miles of ornate crypts and necropolises that could've housed kings they were so massive. The sight was breathtaking. To my left, there were more different graves still. These contained great carved stone statues that appeared to move on their own. As I took in the landscape, it seemed all various cemeteries were pieced together and flowed into one. I had never dreamed this expanse was so enormous and gravely beautiful. I turned back to the pond, and the tip of my shoe caught on something.

I knelt and raked my fingers through the grass. Something sharp pricked my fingertip. I sucked on my injured finger, tasting copper on my tongue, and examined the item I found. Three inches long and curved. It resembled a dog's canine. *Morana said she heard dogs attacking the other reaper. But what kind of canines would attack a reaper?* I slipped the tooth through the folds of my robe and found the pocket of my jeans so I wouldn't lose it. I glanced at my pierced digit and discovered it was still bleeding. I pressed it against my robe and looked down into the cemetery. A bare spot stood out among the rows of crypts. No grass grew in this spot of black earth.

In the middle of the dirt was a single canine imprint.

A light breeze stirred the blades along with a bit of black fabric snagged on a low branch. It waved harder in the gale like a marker pointing me in the right direction. I glanced back where

I left Morana. She hadn't cried out or come after me so I assumed she was safe. A sensation pulled me forward that I couldn't ignore. When I reached for the scrap, the cloth reacted to me as though it were alive. The tendrils of fabric had a life of their own and strained to get back to me. I took the small ribbon and held it.

Pain. Surrounded. Blackness. Something tearing into his flesh and ripping him apart. The last few seconds of his existence melted into my mind. The impression didn't give me a look at who or what attacked him. *There should be been more footprints. Some sign of disturbance, but there's nothing else. The breach within this dimension should've never occurred.* I shoved the fabric into my pocket to show to Azrael. Hopefully, he'd have some answers.

Sometimes it was difficult to locate him. Being my boss, and an Archangel, he had the ability to split his being into a thousand diverse versions of himself across dimension, galaxies, universes, and timelines so he could collect souls. Getting him compressed into one being where he wasn't half distracted was a rare event. Not all reapers ever got as much face time as I had with him. Of course, there were other exceptions. His mate got most of his attention. Her name was Brenna. She assisted me in beating the devil last year by giving me a knife I used on Mastema. Brenna was the equal counterpart of Azrael and worked as a psychic. Brenna practiced in a different dimension, but being a reaper didn't limit her from crossing dimensions. It was like breaking the surface of the water. It was as easy as breathing because, as I had learned, nothing could stop death. It was inevitable.

I guess that meant I was, too.

I saw a bit of movement among the graves. If some animals lurked amid the crypts, I wasn't going to risk being attacked. The evidence I had was enough to show Azrael. I went back to find Morana. The little girl hadn't moved from the lake. She skipped stones along the pond. One skimmed over the water four times before it sank beneath the surface and disappeared.

"That's quite impressive," I said to her.

She jumped and turned around. "My daddy taught me how to do it. Do you think I'll ever see him again?"

"Do you know if he was at your house?"

Morana shook her head. The blue ribbon slipped from her pigtail and fluttered to the ground. I reached down to pick it up, but she grabbed it first. *Why doesn't she want me to pick up her ribbon?* She flashed me an innocent smile. "Mommy said if I lost any more ribbons then I'd be in trouble." She tied the ribbon back around her braid.

I could understand that.

"Did you find what you were looking for?" she asked.

"I saw a paw print that looked like it might have come from a dog. If there were more, they were lost within the grass. Thanks for bringing me here. What about your father? Is he still at your old house?"

"No," she answered. "I don't know where he went. Mommy isn't there, either."

"I can bring you to the mist, and then you can go from there. Maybe he'll meet you on the edge. That happens sometimes. It'll bring you peace."

"What if I don't want to go?"

"Then you don't have to. No one is forcing you to crossover if you don't want to. I just thought you wanted to see your parents again. You—" I stopped when I heard something. The wind ceased. I listened harder. A swoosh, a rustling of the grass and the trees, sounded in the distance.

"Did you hear that?" Her wispy voice came out in a breathy terror filled whisper. She gripped my hand harder until I lost the feeling even in my bone fingers.

The sound came again, followed by a low, menacing guttural growl. It came closer this time. I glanced around, but didn't see anything. More snarls echoed in the eerie stillness of the graveyard. Instinct told me they lingered at the top of the hill, waiting for us to run. Some predatory pack had gotten into the cemetery of souls. *Now I really have to tell Azrael about this.* The wild dogs might have been out for blood, but I wasn't about to die again today.

I summoned all my power and felt my wings open. My stomach quivered with fright. "Hold on." I sensed they had launched down the hill and would be on us in a heartbeat maybe two. Before they could, I stepped with Morana toward the pond and felt the worlds part as I envisioned my house. A raking pain sliced down my back at the last second. I cried out and lost my grip on Morana.

The sudden agony propelled me forward. I landed on my knees in my kitchen instead of my office. Something cold dumped all over my head. I looked up to Than standing over me with a pitcher of empty ice-tea. My cold exterior had fallen away, and the weight of my wings retreated. The tea turned sticky on the back of my T-shirt. My wounds stung as the sugar reacted to the gouges. I spit the rest of the tea out and glanced up at my soul mate.

"What are you doing here? I thought you were writing?"

I forced a smile. "And I thought you were getting lunch."

"I did. I went to that little place in Lamia we found that day when we had to go get those souls of that married couple." He pointed toward the containers on the counter.

Warmth engulfed me, and I fanned myself. When I tried to get up, the pain of the claw marks burned. I couldn't move. "Yeah, great. Food, but I need your help. Get the bandages and the alcohol from the bathroom please."

"Why do you need those? If you're hurt, the wounds will heal."

"Just go." Pain burned along my spine. "I'll explain when you get back."

Than ran into the downstairs bathroom and grabbed the supplies. I had them on hand in just in case. He came back in and helped me get my shirt off. He peeled the fabric away from the scratches. Each small movement made my back a lake of agony.

"What the hell happened to you?" Concern ringed in his voice.

"I was taking a soul over. I was attacked by a pack of wild dogs or something. I gathered what power I could and came back here. I lost the soul. Whatever they are clawed me right before I left."

"How could something get into the soul yard? It's closed off to everyone except reapers and the souls who pass through there." He dabbed at the wounds. I hissed in a breath. "Sorry."

"It's fine." Something dark had rooted in the cemetery if the pack was there. Was the peaceful world I knew crashing to an end?

"How do you think that whatever did this would've gotten into the graveyard?"

"Hell, if I know. How bad are the wounds?"

He grew quiet. I didn't appreciate the silence. Many things could be said about the absence of a comment or sound. Silence was something I understood and rather enjoyed. In death there was great stillness and sometimes there was noise. So loud it was deafening. And sometimes death was unexpected, like today.

"There are four scratches. They don't look too deep, but they're red. They should be healing. Why aren't they?"

"I don't know." I sensed his exasperation as he placed the bandages on my back.

"Maybe we should find Azrael and tell him what's happening."

"You think?" I barked.

"You don't have to snap at me. I know you're hurting, but I'm not going anywhere."

My cellphone rang. Than answered it and knelt before me. "Hello."

"Who is it?" I asked him.

"No, Sparrow. Now really isn't a good time." His brow furrowed. Whatever she said to him meant it was important. "How did you know that?"

I gestured for him to give me the phone which he forked over. I sat up slowly. The fire of my wounds wrapped around my spine as the skin stretched and my muscles moved. "Hello."

"Kerstin, are you okay? I feared the worst."

"Sparrow, what did you see?" She helped me in the past against the serial killer who had tried to get Lucifer into this reality. We stayed in contact over the past couple of years. I wasn't sure if I trusted her enough to consider her a friend, but it was nice to be able to talk to someone who understood what I was.

"You were attacked today. I saw a graveyard. You were with someone I couldn't identify. A howl curdled my blood and broke the silence of the cemetery. And then there was agonizing pain. Are you okay?" Sparrow asked me.

I glanced at Than. Questions lingered in his eyes, and I felt them in his mind from the bond that we shared. My wounds burned, but the agony was less than it had been. I prayed they were healing. "I'll be fine. I think. Yes, I was attacked by something. A pack of wild animals I think. How they got into the graveyard is beyond me. Any idea on that one since you're so in touch with the dead?"

Sparrow sighed. "I've felt a few things. Heard a few things. Not sure what's stirring. Even I don't have full dominion over the dead like you do. I can ask around some more though, maybe summon up something and interrogate it."

"I don't want you torturing a poor spirit into giving you information. Let the dead sleep when they've earned it. Those who have passed on don't deserve to be pulled back unless they chose to and communicate with their loved ones. I mean—"

"Kerstin, I'm not going to awaken those who are already gone by. You don't need to worry about it. I have too much respect for those to wrestle them back. Besides, I'd never do anything to cross my favorite grim reaper. I know better than that. The only ones I was going to torment were the ones still hanging around and want to cause harm. Surely, you don't have any issue with that."

"Never said that I did. So yeah, I guess any information you can find out would be great. In general, have you been feeling that there's something off in the universe?"

"Not exactly the way you might be feeling it. It's almost like raindrops pinging off something metal. I feel the reverberation. It's faint. I can't pinpoint where the ripples are coming from. The first thing I wanted to do was contact you. After the last time we met and well…nothing's going to ever top defeating Lucifer. I still can't get over that I met the Devil."

"Don't count it as lucky. It's best for you to forget all about it and pray Mastema has forgotten all about you. Sparrow, you don't need him hanging around you. Trust me."

"Has he not left you alone?" Static swallowed some of her words, but I made it out. She helped save me from the devil, but no one needed to be on his list. Believe me, I wanted off of it.

I tried to think about my life without the devil whispering in my mind when all I wanted was freedom. "No."

"You did free him from hell."

"No, his minion freed him. I was just the catalyst so he could crossover into this reality."

"All semantics really," she remarked.

"Whatever. Just be glad you're not on his radar. Will you tell me if you find something on your end?"

"Cross my heart. Hope to die. Just promise you'll be my reaper if anything bad happens."

"I seriously doubt it'll come to that, but fine. Let me know what you find out." I hung up and wondered what she would do. The reaper part wanted no part in her tactics on what she would do to a soul. I was supposed to be impartial, but sometimes I couldn't be.

"What did she say?" Than asked.

I relayed her part of the conversion to him and stood up as the pain abated. I glanced at the food. My appetite evaporated. "We need to get Azrael."

"You think that's necessary?"

"Do you really think it's not a good idea to tell the Archangel who rules us?"

"I'm thinking about the welfare of the other reapers. Maybe it's a fluke and the souls of some wild dogs got lost."

I pulled out the tooth and the bit of fabric from my pocket. I plunked them down on the counter. "Tell me that's not enough to prove I'm not wrong."

CHAPTER FOUR

Than didn't answer me. I took a deep breath. The wounds on my back twinged. "I'll see if I can find him."

Than grabbed my shoulder. I scooped up the fabric and the tooth and shoved them back into my pocket. "I'll go. You stay here and eat. Rest. Whatever. We don't know if Azrael's been hurt or if he knows others who have been." Than ran a hand through his hair, pacing around the kitchen.

He spent over two hundred years watching over me. Than was my soulmate, so I knew his pain. Seeing me live and die again without any knowledge of who or what I had been had nearly crippled him. He protected me from an insane grim reaper who wanted to kill me. It was from that encounter that I ended up being a grim reaper.

In the past, I was a grim reaper named Lissandra. Than and Sariel were my reaper team. Then I had screwed it all up because I answered the call of a witch in Death's Dance. I spent human lifetimes dealing with the guilt. After dying, and being resurrected by Azrael, Than had somehow linked my memories to an alternate version of me that lived in this very same house.

The other me was an ordinary psychic and a bestselling author. Sometimes our paths crossed in this house where I saw a shadow of myself or something would've moved. Than had chosen this home for me because it was a nexus. It'd be easier for me to be in touch with my other self to make up for the time that I had been dead and then brought back to life.

Sometimes the semantics were too complicated to think about, but hell...as a reaper I could traverse dimensions, universes, timelines, and worlds with ease. Even though Azrael turned me into a hybrid, I was still me. Now I needed all of me to figure out what was going on. I had no idea what those creatures were in the graveyard.

Taking a shot, I went back into my office and glanced at the couple dozen tarot decks I owned. I closed my eyes and ran my hand a few inches above them. A tingling started in the center of my palm as I passed over the tops of the cards. My hand stopped over the second row of cards. I brought the tarot over to the table and sat down to focus on my question.

I held the cards between my hands, trying to clear my mind. The energy of the cards prickled my palms. The top of my head tingled. My guides filled me with light and expanded my consciousness to a new level. It reminded me there was life after death. Mostly their presence spoke to the human in me and not the reaper. Sometimes I forgot about this aspect of myself and I needed to remember. I wasn't just a reaper. I was also a psychic who helped people.

I shuffled the cards until the urge to stop came over me. I pulled three cards and laid them left to right, face down. The cards had an Egyptian theme because the backs were decorated with hieroglyphics. I trailed my fingers over the first card and flipped it over. The Tower. A pyramid with a bolt of lightning breaking off the top of it. Two figures were falling, face down, toward the ground. The card represented my past. Everything was crumbling down around me. *Yeah, that's already happened. I lost my old house and my life.* All that I knew from being a normal human had crumbled. Because of the destruction, I picked myself back up and figured out a new life. I drummed my fingers over the center of the card and didn't feel anything else coming from it.

The middle card, my present, was the Wheel of Fortune. It was a large wheel in the center of the card with a sphinx sitting on top of it and two demons falling off the wheel. Everything was spinning out of control. The universe was set on its head, and I had nowhere to go. Anything could happen good or bad. It was like playing the supernatural lottery. It all depended on the luck of the draw. Sometimes I could change my lot, and sometimes I could not. This was showing the things I was involved in now. The missing grim reaper. Mastema. Maybe something on a grander scale I hadn't seen yet. Whatever point it would land on I would make a decision. That choice would send out ripples, or the wheel could be collecting them from past mistakes.

Butterflies battered my stomach at the last card. I didn't want to turn it over. It stuck to the velvet table cloth. I forced it to flip over and another card slid off the back of it. I concentrated on this card first. Ten of Swords. Ten blades pointed up on the card with the Eye of Horus in the center, seeing all. The swords represented the element of air. Winds were bringing change. The blades were hardship both mental and physical, being backstabbed and betrayed. To some it was the real death card.

The last card stuck to the Ten of Swords was the Death card. Anubis held canopic jars. He ruled the underworld. Behind him were the scales of balance. Does your soul continue its journey, or does it descend being weighed against the heaviness of the feather? Death was transition. Change.

The cards meaning didn't bode well. I didn't delve into my own future much, but it had to be clearer than this. It wasn't like the world was going to end again. Something had to give me a heads up. Right now, all the cards revealed Death was coming.

CHAPTER FIVE

How could Death be coming?

"It can't come because he's already here."

A seven foot tall figure in a black designer suit stepped from the darkness. An amethyst aura surrounded him and outlined his large wings. They folded into his back and disappeared. His pale skin contrasted with his onyx suit. His midnight eyes reflected universes being born and dying. This was the all mighty Azrael. If I didn't work for him, I would be terrified of the reason why he abruptly materialized in my office.

"Hello, Azrael."

"It's good to see again, Kerstin." He studied the tarot spread and picked up the Death card. A small corner of his mouth turned up into a smile. One of the few times I had seen him show emotion. He set the card back in its place before taking the chair opposite me. "I don't see the likeness, and the hieroglyphics are inaccurate."

"I didn't buy them for that. I find I can only read a tarot deck if I feel an affinity for the Death card."

"You sound like Brenna. She said the same thing about her

cards."

"How is she doing?" In her I felt a kindred spirit but hadn't really had a good chance to talk with her.

"She's well. Her business moved into another location. I'm certain if you ever need a job, she could use a good psychic."

"I'm not sure I could orient myself in a parallel dimension."

"You do it as a reaper."

"True, but I'm not spending a whole lot of time there. Just picking up and dropping off so to speak."

"Good analogy and very true. I can understand this, but here you are, on a nexus of all things where the veils between the worlds are thin. You should be used to the fluctuation of the energies of the other realms."

"On some level, I am. But that doesn't mean I enjoy catching glimpses of another me in the house, or the random sightings of creatures and entities that pop in. About a month ago, I could've sworn I saw Bigfoot running around in the woods, but it could've been my imagination."

His left eyebrow raised. "I doubt it's your imagination. Unless the things you saw in the graveyard were also your imagination?"

"I didn't think you knew about that. Do you know what they are? How they got there? Did Than find you?"

"I don't know what they are or how they got there. No, I haven't seen Than. I have been taking care of other things in the worlds. There is some…unrest brewing among the realms. Sometimes even I can't get away from it. As an Archangel, I'm obligated to quell some disputes no matter where they take me to."

A shiver of dread rolled along my spine. "I'm sure Than's still looking for you. You're not exactly easy to find."

"True. Tell me what happened when you were in the

cemetery."

I glanced at the cards again and told him of my encounter with Morana. I showed him my wounds. His cool fingers ran over the claw marks. They tingled from the touch and heated as his power flashed through me. It healed whatever was left of the scratches. When I checked my pricked finger, it was healed as well. Only he could bring such a gift, holding the power of life and death because of his station. I pulled out the tooth and the scrap of robe.

The fabric squirmed in his palm, inching closer to his sleeve. It wove in with his shirt. Azrael shivered and closed his eyes. He winced. A soft moan slipped from his lips. I quivered hearing the sound because it chilled me to the core. His eyes snapped open. The awesome power of his gaze fell upon me. In those penetrating midnight eyes, I saw all of him instead of him being scattered around the universes. The muscles in Azrael's jaw clenched. He curled his hands into a fist. A bit of red appeared in his eyes before it faded away. "This belonged to Sampson. He was one of the very first reapers I assigned to collect souls. Which part of the necropolis did you find this in again?"

"The tombs were ancient. Large graves almost like small temples with the way the pillars were. Some were a mixture of Egyptian and Greek. Maybe Roman. A place I hadn't been to before."

"That was Sampson's part all right. Each reaper shapes their portion of the graveyard. They intersect, but not many reapers go between them. If all you found was this…" His words died as he pulled the scrap from his shirt and wove it through his fingers.

"You felt what happened to him. I saw the pain flash across your face. I experienced it too when I picked it up."

"Yes. I relived the echo of his suffering, but I don't know

what went after him. It sounds like a feral canine. The tooth also provides evidence of that. Maybe some animal spirit was loosened in the cemetery. How do you feel about going back in and investigating this creature?"

"Really? You want me to go up against something that can kill me? I don't want to die again."

He glared at me, and his mouth tightened. "True, but if these creatures are capable of killing reapers, then it's best we know exactly what they are so we can dispose of them. You aren't a true reaper anymore. You're something in between that no one has seen before. You are neither human nor reaper. The scratches you had were healing slowly. I have a feeling if left they would've festered. This wound to a reaper could kill them."

"Azrael, no disrespect, but if I get a direct hit with a scythe or a sickle I'm toast. You can't bring me back. I don't want to be involved in a life-threatening situation again. I enjoy my life as it is."

"I understand your trepidation, but you're in a unique position. You have some idea of what we're looking for. I can give you the added support of a warrior angel or two. Would that satisfy you? I don't want to order you to do this, even though I could."

"I know you can." I glanced at the cards one more time. *Is this where the wheel of fortune stopped? Are the ripples of my decisions catching up to me?* Azrael wasn't going to let me get off easily. It'd been my decision to bring this to Azrael because I didn't want other reapers dying. It didn't matter if he forced me to do this or not. I'd already made the decision to get involved. "Just promise me this. When I figure this out, that's it. You leave me alone for a while and give Than some time off, so I can spend it with him."

He smiled, showing his long sharp canine teeth. "That I will happily guarantee. But if I recall, you brought this to me. I do promise, however, you will not be the bait as you were last time."

"Then we have a deal. Can I ask you something?"

"One question, and then I must go."

"How can you be both a vampire and an Archangel? You were human once like Brenna. It's something I've always wondered."

Azrael trailed his fingers over the tarot deck and took them in his hands. He shuffled a few times and separated them into three different piles. He tapped a finger over all three before deciding to flip the cards over. My forehead tingled at the advice my guides wanted to give to the dark angel.

He pulled the World. Judgment. The Moon.

The World card had the Eye of Horus at the top of the card, looking down on the person. A bird flew upward toward the unknown. It meant that the world was open to all different kinds of things. There were a ton of different possibilities. It was the start of new things. This was all the past. It had to mean Azrael being presented with a new life. But which one? The existence of a vampire or the one of an angel?

Judgment was next. Anubis leading someone into the underworld. Death judging all sins. Having to face the things that have come before, the past coming back to haunt him.

The future card was the Moon. A full moon hung between two pyramids. On each side were two different dogs. Black and white. The moon represented the path to rid one's self of deceptions, put aside all pretenses. What you think you see is not really what you're seeing. The road you walk is blocked by illusion and sacrifices. Intuition has to be the guide. If you can't see the true path then you might not be walking on it. Sometimes the right decision seems the most perilous.

How does this play into his future? I wasn't sure if the reading was Azrael or for me.

He set his hand over the middle pile. I slid my hand over his. His skin was cool under the warmth of my palm, and his power collided with my own. His was far greater. I could never see into the vastness of how much he encompassed. The heaviness of prophecy fell over me. My eyes closed of their own accord. My guides were persistent. A massive energy wave stung my entire body as though I had been hit with an electrified whip. This otherness consumed me, a life-giving force coursed through me and the exact opposite of the death energy.

The otherness stepped into my consciousness and pushed me aside. My boss tried to pull his hand from mine, but my strength was no rival to his.

"If you wish an answer then let go," he said simply.

Instead of seeing the mighty angel, I saw the vampire behind the cool facade. Black eyes with red pupils glowed from within his twisted face. His lips were pulled back in a perverse grin, showing a double set of canine teeth, covered with blood. Flashes of people's faces flickered in my mind, and the enjoyment and sheer abandon buried in his soul overwhelmed me. However, he was set apart from the other vampires. They could become this other beast, and it had a different personality than the host. The undead originated from Mastema. The vampires were his children. I caught glimpses of my boss bowing before Lucifer and him transforming into a serpent, losing who he was bit by bit. Brenna saved him. There were other hints of an epic battle between him and other archangels and creatures. At the end, I sensed being surrounded by death in all stages, sizes, and personalities. This cool energy helped ease the burning energy within me, but the personality within my thoughts burned brighter.

"You turn the cards and summon the fates."

"I call for no such advice. The vessel here is one you've chosen to come into. You are the one who has chosen to impart a message when I didn't seek out your council."

"Always the calm one, Azrael, even when you were given the choice to elevate to your current status."

"Who are you, and why do you inhabit one of my reapers?" He tried once more to pull his hand from my grasp.

"One who wishes the natural order of things is kept. This receptacle is not *just* yours. You gave her a tie to life by keeping her soul intact and letting her walk into places that have been in shadow. You *chose* to give her a slice of life beyond what was owed. That makes her unique, but you already know this."

"The choices I made can't be undone. What is your message?" Azrael growled.

The frigid cold of his power rivaled the warmth flowing into me. The entity in me seemed amused. "My message is this. The past isn't so easily forgotten no matter how much one makes amends. Sometimes the events set in motion can reopen old wounds. No one is free from this. The consequences of all our decisions can be dire."

"Tell me exactly what I should be looking out for."

I leaned closer. "Who said this message was just for you? This place has doorways where many can press their ear up to it and hear what's being said." The overpowering entity left me. I released Azrael's hand and fell back into my seat. I closed my eyes and rested my head on the back of the chair to regain my bearings.

"Are you okay?"

I opened my eyes and saw my boss's concern. The images of him being a vampire lingered. They gave me some more insight into Azrael's past. "Fine. Thanks. Someone wanted to talk to you."

"It seems so, but I think the communication was for both of us. Do you have any idea what or who came through?"

"No. Sometimes I can figure it out, but this being had me blocked off. They showed me images of you being a vampire. You enjoyed it, and you're different from the others."

"True. I'm different than the breed that I'm a part of. As you know, different realities beget different choices and monsters."

"Of course." Every reality a reaper crossed into was unique. "You became a vampire and loved it."

"The woman who made me wanted me at her side even when I turned out unlike all the others. Most live with the beast and do anything for their master. Some fight with the other personality. Those are weak and exterminated. Some lose their humanity altogether. I glorified in the killing for a time. Then I realized it was wrong and wanted to repent. I stopped murdering and took what I needed. Sometime later I was given a choice to become the Angel of Death. The angelic part of me made it easier to deny the vampire unless I spent some time on Earth. Then the hunger was awakened. I remained aloof, collecting souls, directing those under me, until I met Brenna. She made me remember who and what I was. For five thousand years, I've been this. Then she changed my world."

"It must've been tough going from being a vampire to an angel. That's two extremes."

"It was. Not all who were told of my ascension were pleased about it."

"How so?"

His cool demeanor returned. "That's ancient history. Back to your mission. I'll send two warrior angels to look after you while you investigate Sampson's disappearance."

"Thank you. I'd rather have them here before I venture back

into the cemetery."

"Wise choice. I'll send them soon. If I see Thanatos, I'll direct him home, informing him we have already spoken."

"Thanks."

The room was already empty, and the rift in the universe sealing behind my boss. *Typical.* The wind chimes in the other room sounded again. I gathered the cards and restacked them into a pile. A cool breeze wrapped around me when I went into the living room. It didn't raise goose bumps on my flesh. All my senses told me someone was in the house with me. After what happened in the graveyard, I wasn't going to take any chances. I summoned my scythe. My fingers curled around the smooth wood, and it brought me comfort.

"I know you're there. Come out."

The door slowly inched open. A young man in his early twenties stood behind it. Black hair stuck out from under a ball cap. The golden hat was smudged with blood. He was dressed in a dark blue and golden baseball uniform. Small gold hoops in both his ears caught the light. He had pale golden skin with flat black eyes. In one hand he had a baseball glove also stained a dark brown.

"Who are you?" I asked.

"Are you one of them? Because you don't look like them or even feel like them." It sounded as though he was from New York, but I wasn't making any assumptions.

"One of who?"

"The dudes in the Halloween costumes. One minute I was at home gettin' ready for the game. The next I was standin' over myself with these two dudes dressed in long black cloaks. I couldn't see their faces, but they said they were there to take me home. I didn't want to go at first. They told me I was dead and I couldn't go back to my body. They showed me what happened. Arty, that no good son of a bitch, slugged me from behind. He always wanted my spot on the team. I said yes to the guys. They take my hands, and we were in this cemetery. All of a sudden somethin' was growlin' behind us. One of them faced it, and the other kept leadin' me sayin' it was fine. Then I hear screamin'."

"What happened?"

He shrugged. "The other one told me to go through the fog. He had a curved blade like you got and went back to help the other one. I heard another shriek, and saw a streak of black in the distance. I ran among the graves and found this little girl. She told me to come find Kerstin. Are you Kerstin?"

This wasn't good.

Another lost soul came to me because two more reapers had been attacked. Sampson's attack wasn't a solitary incident. "I'm Kerstin. Could you bring me back to where the reapers took you?"

He nodded, and his cap tumbled to the floor. I vanished the scythe and picked up his hat. The emblem was a picture of a donkey or maybe a buffalo. His fingers brushed along mine when I handed it back to him. A slight blush ran along his cheeks, and he pulled his fingers away. He settled it back on his head and turned it. Clumps of hair were matted with brain matter and his skull.

"Raj. I don't want to go back there."

I laid a hand on his arm. "I know, but I have a duty to protect the other reapers and find out what's doing all of this."

"You their protector or somethin'?"

"Something like that. We reapers have to stick together. If something is running around in the cemetery, then it's unsafe for them as it is for the people we bring to the other side. I'd appreciate your assistance."

"I can't go back there right now. I saw the beasts tearin' apart one of those dudes. It grew dark, and the shadows became long. I heard them comin' after me, too, as I ran further into the graveyard. It wasn't until I saw the little girl, who sent me to you, that I knew I had a chance. She said you were a little different."

"Did she say when she'd come back?"

"No, just that I'd find you in a house in the middle of the woods. I got to your old boneyard there, and the other spirits there told me you were inside."

"At least they were helpful. I can offer you food and rest if that's what you wish."

"Food? I can eat even though I'm dead?"

"In this place and because of who I am, yes. Feel free to raid my fridge, but stay out of my bedroom and my office. Another reaper lives here with me. He has blond hair. If you see him, please let me know."

Raj's eyes widened. "Another reaper. Okay. Uh…can I order a pizza?"

I rolled my eyes. "Check out the fridge or freezer first. If you don't find anything in there that satisfies you, I'll order a pizza."

I left the living room and slipped outside. A lot had happened in the day, and I hadn't had a chance to catch my breath. More questions needed to be answered. Than hadn't returned home. He could have gotten an assignment. Than could be gone for days or weeks. It all depended on how many souls he had to collect. At times Than got caught up or had another reaper to help him. He would show up eventually.

Azrael's words rang in my mind. I didn't have a choice. I didn't want to know what my boss would do with me if I didn't fulfill his orders.

CHAPTER SIX

Raj had a hefty appetite, so I ordered two pizzas. I was hungry as well. He binged on television and anything in my fridge. I retreated to my bedroom and stared out at the forest, watching the small globes of light. They floated above the tree tops. They bobbed in and out of the treeline. The lights were said to be lost spirits of women who tried to find their way back to the husbands they had lost. Many didn't know what they were. Some thought they were balls of gas, and others thought they were extraterrestrials. People came from all over to watch the lights. Some had wandered onto my property, so I had to shoo them away.

If they were souls, then they had not called out to me for release. I tended to think the orbs were a natural phenomenon. Maybe they were fairies lost in the storms between realms, and they couldn't get out. Whatever they were, they made this region a little famous.

"Does it truly matter if they're balls of condensed methane or if they're something more?" The smooth voice whispered in my mind. "They do say the devil is in the details."

I didn't need someone else in my head. "Why can't you leave me alone?"

"Because deep down you don't *want* me to leave you alone. You long to have me there with you." He slid his arm around my waist. His passion stirred an undeniable urge within me, and a deep buried part did want him there. It yearned to part the realms and smuggle him into mine. Although that was the lust talking. I had never actually been to Heaven or Hell, because I wasn't allowed to go that far. I gazed into Mastema's dimension. It was a shadowy place of unsung dreams and torture. I wished I could've released the innocent souls of those who didn't belong there. We were able to free the souls of those who had fueled doorway that he used to try and step through into this realm. It had angered him, but…

"But I never used it against you. Besides, I forgave you after a while. You're such a marvelous creature. I don't know if I could ever say no to you. Speaking of which, I still owe you that boon. Anything you wished for, I can give it to you." His velvet voice touched upon my flesh like a soft caress.

I shivered. "That's not going to happen. You don't have anything I want. Stop trying to entice me. Go away. I don't need you in my head right now."

"You could've fooled me. I know you're longing for that dark angel of yours. Your love for him reaches across time. You're more powerful than you give yourself credit for, than even Azrael gives you credit for. He never should've locked you back into the world of life and death."

"That's his decision and not mine."

"You could've chosen to move on into the other realm. You deserved it. If you had, none of this would be happening."

I squeezed my eyes shut and covered my ears, trying to force him from my mind. His presence didn't retreat. Mastema slid his arms up my sides and cupped my breasts. His silky lips trailed along the curve of my neck. I held in a breath and squeezed my thighs together. Everything in me screamed not to let the devil win, but sometimes it was so tough to fight him. All he wanted me to do was to ask him for the boon. If he granted it, there would be no going back. I would be his. I didn't want to be the angel forced into hell. I wasn't going to turn my back on the man I loved. He nipped at my throat. My entire body was set on edge as he bit down a little harder. A small moan escaped from my lips.

"This isn't my fault. How could I have anticipated grim reapers going missing or these strange beasts roaming the cemetery?"

"You tipped the world off kilter when you released Sariel, that insane reaper of yours, back into this world. Because you corrected that mistake tumblers twirled in locks. The actions of others created a series of events culminating in this very thing you're investigating. If you'd just chosen to release Sariel, and moved on... this might not be happening. Others are to blame for this, too, and my return. Do you really think my return to this world was to bring a hell on Earth? You know better than that, Kerstin."

He hinted at something, but he always played two sides, threading a little bit of truth in with believable lies. "So make my life easier. Impart your infinite wisdom, and tell me what's going on."

Mastema clutched my breasts and squeezed them until the longing in me burned so hot it felt like I'd ignite. The heat he infected me with clashed with the cold of my office. The two warring sensations nearly sent me over the edge into an orgasm. I fought the pleasure. "Is that the boon you wish of me? To answer your questions and lay this whole scenario out to you? If that is what you truly desire, then all you have to do is say so."

He flicked his tongue along my throat and released my breasts, trailing his fingers down my sides until I shook with unspent desire. His fingers played over the waistband of my jeans and stopped. I struggled to breathe as his words rang in my ear. My heart hammered along my ribcage.

He could tell me exactly what was happening.

I opened my eyes when Mastema inched his fingers a tad lower. He felt more corporeal than before. I glanced down and saw the outline of an arm around my waist. His fingers were solid with tan skin and long dark pointed nails. I screamed and wound my way out of his grasp. I turned back around. His laughter filled the room as he wiggled his fingers at me and pulled his arm back through the dimensional rift.

"What the fuck was that? I thought you couldn't pass through to this side. You were supposed to be closed off in hell."

"Who said anything about me being completely imprisoned? You think there isn't another door that I can't step through or other parts of the universe where I can't become a little bit solid. Oh, Kerstin, if you truly let me into your heart, then I can be all that you crave. I can show you what you can do with that magnificent body. You wouldn't have to ever worry about that dark angel. You'd cry out my name and beg me to bring you the darkest pleasure."

"Get out, Mastema. I don't want you here. Your silken words and stolen kisses might distract me for a few minutes, but I'm never going to let you step into this world."

"Suit yourself. But this won't get any easier. Not everyone agrees with what Azrael has done. Did it ever occur to you your beloved boss has angered a few of the wrong people?"

His presence dissipated, and the atmosphere returned to normal. I dismissed what he said. My hands shook from the encounter. I rolled my shoulders to push the idea of his touch away. *Mastema's messing with me, pure and simple.* I glanced back outside and the orbs undulated in my backyard. They drifted closer to the house. They winked in and out. The television sounded downstairs, so I knew Raj was occupied. The lights continued their wild romp. *Maybe they're trying to get my attention. It wouldn't be the first time something strange happened.*

I willed myself outside underneath the lights. Birds twittered and frogs croaked. The lights danced around my head in a frenzy.

"Okay, I'm out here. What do you want?"

Once I asked, they droned as loud as a bee. "Enough buzzing around already. If you want me to follow you, then lead the way."

The swarm circled around me once more and shot off into the woods. I couldn't keep up with them so flying was easier. The tips of my wings brushed against the tree trunks, shaking the leaves from the branches. Soon I was so deep in the woods the trunks were too close together. I dropped back to the ground. The orbs stopped. They led me to the side of a mountain that didn't appear to have any human habitation for miles around. The darkness revealed a broken-down house rotting in a small clearing a few feet away. The largest globe of light darted into the building, and the others followed behind it. No trees had fallen on the roof. Ivy slithered up the walls. Small tree limbs forked out of the bottom windows. The chimney crumbled, dumping bricks along the side of it. Branches broke under foot. The noise exploded a string of chimney swifts from the top of the chimney. The globes of light gave off enough illumination I could see a few feet before me. I glanced around and didn't see any sign of a road. The front door hung half on its hinges, and part of it was

45

missing. The boards screamed under my weight. I followed the orbs into the foyer. These spheres merged into one large ball filling the space with a soft warm glow. Before me was a staircase. The landing and stairs had fallen in. I flew to the top floor. Graffiti covered the wood. Empty beer bottles were scattered around the floor. The large ball zoomed down the hall and shot into a room. I shielded my eyes from the glow.

"Hello," I addressed it.

It vibrated in a low hum I couldn't understand. With each word or squeak it grew brighter until the warmth fanned across my skin.

"Whoa. I get you're trying to tell me something, but I can't make it out."

The glow muted and I saw the outline of a woman. She was small, about four feet tall with long flowing blond hair. Her eyes were pale gold. When her light dissipated, she appeared human enough. Her energy was more than a spirit and more than angel. *What are you?*

"Can you understand me now?"

Her dress flared out hiding her feet. Although there was no breeze, it fluttered, showing a bit of black mixed among the white. We were in our own little pocket of the world. "Yes."

She smiled. The left side of her face fell way revealing half a skull underneath. When she moved, her beautiful exterior had returned. Something about her was familiar.

"Do you know who I am?"

"No. Sorry. I know you're not an angel. You're definitely not a spirit. So you have to be something in between."

The right side of her face faded to reveal a dark hole where her eye was. The rest of her face remained beautiful. Her feet touched down on the floorboards. The room transformed into a stone cavern with fires flaring around me. A large silver caldron sat between us. Behind her was a massive stone throne. Jets of fire spurted up at various times through the fissures in the floor. She passed her hand over the caldron.

"Have you figured out who I am yet? What I am?"

"Someone who likes to entertain people with a light show?"

"That was only to blend in. The others can't know I'm here."

"What others?" We were the only ones in this barren place. Behind the throne appeared a crumbling ruin of a temple. This location had once been something of grandeur. I could see how it used to be. All at once the echoes of the past came alive around me as if an old movie started playing. People walked through a doorway of light in the temple. The woman stood before the throne and directed the people into the light. Others gathered around the caldron. Before I could make any sense of it, the vision vanished. This creature was something more than what I was. Maybe even something more than what Azrael was, and I didn't think that was possible.

"I have little time here. You must be careful. The old one has arisen."

"Old one?"

"You should know him. He reigned over what we are."

Her words didn't make any sense. I tried to get my bearings, but this place was full of memories. It would make my life easier to crack the riddle I had fallen into. "I'm sorry, but I don't know who you're talking about or who you are."

"You're unique, and the only one who can stop him. Don't let the others fool you. Only you can see what they really are. Others only see what they wish them to see. Look beyond the physical."

The woman burst into several balls of light before I could

ask her more questions. They swirled around me until the world teetered. I found myself back in the ramshackle house when the light cleared. The room was empty. I shook my head in disbelief, trying to understand all of it. *She came to warn me, but who is this old one? Who can only I see?* I left the room and jumped off the stairs, letting my wings catch my fall. I glanced around the main room trying to gather some evidence of the former inhabitants of the building, but nothing.

"There you are. I was looking all over for you."

Morana stood outside the threshold of the house. The wound in her throat was livider than before. The purple circles under her eyes darkened. Her left eye had glazed over to become milky white. I placed my hand on her head. "Are you feeling okay?"

"I feel fine. I'm hungry though. Can we get some more cookies?"

"Sure."

Her smile revealed a couple of gaps where her teeth had been before. Something was wrong with her. "Thank you. Momma never let me eat junk food. She said it'd rot my teeth."

She wove her small fingers through mine. Her clammy skin repulsed me. "You don't have to worry about that now. You'll see your mother again soon, and you can finally be at peace instead of stuck here."

We walked through the woods and arrived at my boneyard. A few of the souls were revenants, flashes of what they used to be playing over and over again. A handful were phantasms like Morana who wished to remain on the land they were born on. One such ghost was Sarah. Tonight, she floated by the outskirts of the cemetery. Sarah's hair was done up in a tight knot on her head. The color of her dress was tough to make out because she was hazier than usual. She wrung her hands in the material of her skirt. Her headstone revealed she was only twenty when she died. Morana released my hand.

"Sarah, is everything okay?"

She drifted closer. The fright in her eyes worried me. I don't think she'd been this panicked since her life. "Something big and menacing was prowling the graveyard. I think it was looking for you."

"Do you know what it is? What did it look like?"

"I don't know. I was watching the lights and heard it in the woods. This fetid aroma came with it. I heard a scream. It was someone alive. I-I don't think it was good for them. Then the smell came here. It was a shadow with red, soulless eyes. Those eyes were inhuman. I think it was a demon."

Demon. Yeah, that didn't sound good. *Mastema must've sent something after me.* He wasn't going to stop until I gave in. "I'll figure out what it is. Did it come into the graveyard at all?" My gaze swept the darkness, searching for any sign of this creature.

"No. I wasn't sure it could because this is consecrated ground. It was awfully close to the edges though."

"I'll check it out. Morana, stay here with Sarah. If this is a hell beast, then you're safe in the graveyard."

"Please don't leave me alone," Morana whimpered. "I don't want it to get me."

I knelt down and forced a smile, trying to hide my own trepidation. "You have nothing to worry about here. I have a feeling it's after me and no one else. If it can't cross into the cemetery, then you have nothing to worry about."

"You'll come back?"

"I promise. Then we'll make some cookies or whatever you want. Okay?"

"Okay."

I stood up and ruffled her hair before heading back into the woods. As I wandered further back, the night got creepier. It wasn't bad enough I had been transported to some otherworldly dimension by a powerful spirit I couldn't register what she was. Now I was chasing a monster in the woods. *Why do I always get myself into situations like this? Why can't I have a relaxing night, sitting before the fire, reading a good book, or even finishing the book I'm writing? Oh yeah. I'm a grim reaper, and my unlife was never supposed to happen.* I forged ahead. It was all worth it in the end because I got to spend time with Than. If I didn't do it, then Azrael would pluck my wings. It wasn't like I didn't enjoy being a reaper or whatever the hell I was now. Why did my death have to be more complicated than my life?

Deeper into the woods, a light dipped as though someone fell. Footsteps thrashed through the brush. A scream split the silence of the night. After that a blood curdling shriek, the mixture of a screech owl, and something I'd never heard before erupted in the darkness. I raced toward the scream.

"Help," a woman begged.

Another howl pierced the night. This was no ordinary animal. I reached the helpless woman.

"Can you help me?" she pleaded.

I kept an eye out for whatever that was stalking her. Somewhere in the darkness I could feel the gritty presence watching us. I wasn't about to let my guard down. The woman's leg was bent at an odd angle. Her flashlight's meager light flickered. A dark blob crossed the beam. It prowled outside of the beam's reach. The shape grew at least five feet long and four feet tall in the shape of a canine on steroids with the grace of a lion. Its hackles were raised. The woman grabbed my arm.

"It's coming. Please, you have to get out us out of here. It's already killed Gary."

So that was the first scream I heard. I helped her stand as she leaned on me. "What were you doing out here?"

"We were camping and wanted to see the lights. Last night we watched the little orbs dance, and it was wonderful. Tonight, it started about an hour after the lights came out. At first it was fine then sounds echoed from the woods. We thought it was, you know, an owl or a bear even, maybe a mountain lion. Gary brought his rifle just in case. He saw movement in the shadows. He lifted his rifle to shoot, but it pounced on him before he could get a shot off. It tore into him…and I-I- started running. I couldn't see where I was going and then… I think my leg's broken."

The flashlight winked in and out again. The monster growled. It got closer, but stayed out of the light. There was nothing I could do for her here. I had to get back to the house. I couldn't carry her. The only way to do it would be to reveal what I truly was. I didn't have a choice. Whatever this monster was, it would pounce once the light died. I wasn't about to meet it in the dark.

"I can get you out of here, but you can't ask any questions about what you see. Do you understand?"

"Yeah. Sure. Whatever."

I picked her up. The light died. The temperature dropped. The creature had the perfect opportunity. I locked my gaze on it. Its gold eyes flashed in the darkness like embers in the night. A heartbeat passed. Moonlight broke through the canopy and caught the beast in its rays, showing off its gleaming fangs. Its maw widened into a smile. Another heartbeat.

It charged.

"Oh God! It's coming. Go. Go. Go."

It was coming, but I wanted to see if the beast was the same thing that attacked the reapers. The woman beat on my shoulders urging me to run. If this thing did have the ability to truly kill me, I needed to know. Its features blended in with the darkness. Its eyes burned in the night. The undulating shadows showed its bunched muscles as it charged. Air rippled around it as it disappeared and reappeared a few feet from where it had been before. I held my breath as it drew nearer. I was not going to show it my fear. I was not going to let it know how much it shook me. Right when it was about to pounce, I let my wings carry me back to my house. An echoing howl erupted in the night because its prey had escaped. I set the girl down and opened the door. She leaned against the doorway until I could help her inside the kitchen. I pulled out the first aid kit and examined her leg. There was blood from some deep cuts. Her pants were torn, but it didn't look like anything was broken.

"What was that thing?" the woman asked.

"I don't know. What's your name?" I wiped at her flesh with an alcohol pad. She sucked in a breath as I went over a wound.

"Sheri. Johnston. Fuck that hurts."

Dirt smeared across her face. Twigs and dried leaves stuck out every which way from her blond hair. Her blue eyes were swollen from crying, and her cheek smeared with blood. I wiped a little bit of the dirt away and noticed her slash near her temple. "Sheri, you were lucky. That thing was going to do some serious damage to you."

"Tell me something I don't know. By the way, how did we get here so fast? I was deep in the woods, and I didn't see any lights nearby."

She hissed when I poked at her head with another alcohol pad. "I told you not to ask questions. Just be glad I was able to get you out of there alive." I grabbed the phone and dialed emergency services to come and get her. "The ambulance will be here shortly."

"I-I can't leave Gary. He's all alone out there with that thing."

"Gary isn't coming back. You and I both heard his scream. That was the voice of a dying man. You said you saw your companion go down, and he didn't get back up. Believe me when I tell you I have some experience when it comes to the dying."

"Are you some kind of serial killer?" Sheri tried to get up out of the chair, but sunk back into the seat. Her eyes were wild with fright.

"Really? You think I'm going to hurt you after I brought you into my home? I—" My remarks were cut off by a siren. I glanced out the window and saw the red lights of the ambulance coming up the driveway. "Hold on. The ambulance is here." I opened the door while they were parking. I beckoned them into the house through the front door. I even flipped the porch light on so they could see. The garage light winked in and out. A large shadow passed by the side of the driveway weaving between the trees. My heart nearly stopped. The paramedics were getting their gear out of the back of the ambulance and about to come rushing to the house. The light flashed once more. A low growl reverberated in the night.

It stopped in the treeline and peered directly at me. The way its head moved I saw the shadow beast's mouth twisted into a knowing smile. "Is everything okay? Are you the one who is hurt?" one of the paramedics asked me.

I shook my head. Before I could answer the creature leapt from the shadows. It wrapped its paws around the other EMT's shoulders and dragged him down to the ground. He screamed when those powerful jaws sunk into the poor man. Blood spurted on the side of the white and blue ambulance, smearing it red. His partner turned back to assist his friend. I tried to warn him, but I was motionless.

"What's going on?" Sheri yelled from the kitchen.

The beast looked up from its meal and spit the head out so it rolled under the ambulance's front right wheel. The other EMT dropped to his knees. The monster swiped at him with a paw the size of a frying pan. It had the outline of a hyena mixed with a lion. Its snout was more wolf like. If this wasn't a hell beast then I didn't know exactly what it was. Certainly, Mastema sent it to plague my existence.

It met my eyes and pawed the EMT. It caught his chest and spun him around as he fell face down onto the ground. He convulsed. The shadow beast stepped on top of his back holding him in place. The sky opened up. Rain poured down onto the driveway washing away the blood. The monster turned the other man over and pushed its snout into his stomach. A large bite of intestines and organs hung out of its mouth. It swallowed its meal and went back in for more meat. The crunch of bones twisted my stomach. I was powerless to help this man. Fear had me in its hard grip. I knew it could kill me.

An ear-splitting shriek burst behind me. I turned quick enough to hear a thud. Sheri had passed out on the hallway floor. I turned back and saw it come onto the lawn, but stay out of the reach of the porch light. It had more substance to it than it had before. Maybe because it had eaten.

I heard a moan and then another one behind the beast. The two men were looking down at their bodies. Their transparent souls grew solid. The cold power of the reaper crept up within me. The creature before me glanced back at them and chuckled. Its hellish gaze settled on me. It took another step closer to the house. The porch light blinked. I gripped the doorway. Splinters dug under my nails. This close, I saw the definition of glossy fur. Blood slicked its snout. The cruelty and evil in its eyes was something I had not witnessed before. The way it licked its lips and cleaned the meat from its teeth with such purpose; it had to be a creature of the devil. I looked at the souls once more. They lingered around their bodies, lost and wondering what had happened to them. I took one step toward them, overcoming some of the terror that held me in place. The beast stepped in front of me.

"I wouldn't do that if I were you," it said.

"You can talk."

"I can do much more than speak."

"Really? And attacking two helpless men was more than that?" I crossed my arms over my chest.

"I was hungry. They're only the beginning. Those two are a message."

"What message?"

The porch light dimmed until it hung around me like a halo. With one leap he could easily take me down. "You've got one chance to make the right decision."

"What decision is that? Step off the porch and choose to be eaten by you?"

The thing chuckled and shook his head much like a dog would when trying to dry off. "Cute, but no. I have no penchant for dead things. My master's taken a liking to you. Make the correct decision, and you will be spared. Next time I see you, it won't be on such amicable terms."

Listening to the smug beast, more of my fright drained away. I remembered who and what I was. I stepped off the porch away from whatever protection the light afforded me. "You wanted to deliver a message. It would have been easier to step out of the shadows and just tell me."

"This way was more satisfying. And it got your attention. I was hungry. It's been a long time since I've been here. From what I heard about you, I thought you'd have a little more fight in you. The great grim reaper is nothing more than a scared human. Just think on what I said, little girl. The next time it won't be so pleasant for you."

He turned and disappeared into the night. I didn't know what to make of the creature except it was something from my nightmares.

Sheri moaned. The souls of the two paramedics remained. It was my job to take them into the graveyard. After all, it was my fault they had died. I picked Sheri up and brought her to the couch. From there I dialed 911 again and explained a wild animal had attacked. I left Sheri and hoped she would stay unconscious for a little while. Once I knew that the police were on their way, I stepped outside and went to the paramedics. The real world began to lose a little substance. I went to the one who had lost his head. Unlike the other two spirits who I was feeding, these two did not take on the appearance of their death. They remained normal.

"Holy shit. What's happening?" the first paramedic whimpered.

I touched his shoulder and hoped the calming influence of my station would infect him. Sometimes it was easier to take souls when they were still confused. They accepted the idea they were still dead. "It's going to be okay."

He looked at me. I felt his loss set in as he realized what had happened. "That's me, isn't it?"

"Yes. I'm sorry that I have to be the one to tell you."

"We're dead. That thing killed us," the other paramedic

responded.

"You are. Come on. I can bring you peace. Will you come with me?" I offered both of them my hands. They looked at one another and took them after a minute. Once they had my hands, we flew through the dimensions until we were at the entrance to the graveyard that I frequented. I looked around and tried to see if anything was amiss. I didn't feel like there was any rabid animals waiting to pounce on me.

"What is this place?" one of them inquired.

"Is this heaven?" the other asked.

"No. It's not heaven." The question came many times. "It's a place where you have to pass through before you get to where you're going. Follow me."

They squeezed my hands tighter as we walked along one of the dirt paths. Nothing happened, but I kept a lookout for something that might jump out and eat me. We arrived at the wall of fog. The shapes of spirits lingered on the other side of the mist waiting for the two men.

"What's on the other side?" one asked.

"Nothing bad. Just step through, and you'll be reunited with your loved ones."

"Have you ever been on the other side?"

"A few times when I was human, and then reincarnated. Grim reapers aren't allowed to cross, but you'll be fine. Go ahead." I gestured they go ahead of me. Their fear was evident by the shaky looks they gave me, but they stepped into the fog. I waited until they were completely gone before I turned and glanced at the lines of stones that stretched into forever. The longer I stared, the more I could see the different seams of reality, where the various graveyards came together. I was surprised I hadn't seen them. Seeing nothing menacing among the stones, I decided it was okay to wander. I chose a paved path with large cracks in some sections. Most of the markers were black or gray stone. Their faces were blank.

Azrael said these soul yards were the reflections of the reaper. Most are soulless angels who don't understand emotion. A few were once human who retained their souls. Some angels begin to feel so they end up with a soul or at least part of one. That was what happened to Than when I met him. Than was not unfeeling. And then I ruined the whole arrangement and decided to go to Death's Dance.

We all know how that fiasco ended up.

As I walked among the stone sentinels, I contemplated the events that brought me to this point. Sariel found me through Jackson and wanted to kill me because of past events. Than and I freed Death's Dance of the curse that hovered over it. I died, was offered the position of reaper, and reunited with Than. Things were great until Azrael made me human again, messing with the natural order of things. All of a sudden, the two years I'd been dead didn't matter. Than rearranged the details of the timelines. Azrael needed me as bait for drawing out the devil's serial killer. Mastema offered me a once in a lifetime deal to do one thing for me no strings attached as he put it. But who could believe the Devil? The serial killer kidnapped me, gained my blood, and almost my soul. That enabled Mastema to partially come through into this reality. Then I died again, and he was sent back to hell. Azrael reinstated me as a reaper, but I was some weird form of a hybrid. I had all my reaper powers and my psychic ones, too. I walked the line between life and death because my heart still beat.

Anyway, here I was some weird mixture. *Mastema alluded to this messing with the fabric of the universe. So had the spirit who pulled me into her realm. She said I could see what others couldn't. What does this all have to do with reapers disappearing? What is this large beast? It has to do with Mastema giving me ultimatums.* I shouldn't have been scared of the thing, but it shook me to the core. Something like that shouldn't scare a reaper. I don't remember being afraid of anything. Sure a few things could kill us. The scythe we carried. The sickle the serial killer had last year. The beasts hunting the reapers. Azrael healed me of their wounds, but there was more to it. If they could hurt, or even kill a reaper then they had to be associated with death on some level.

"Hello," someone called to me.

He didn't look like a soul in need. I walked to him slowly. He might not have been a ghost, but that did not mean he wasn't an agent of Mastema's. The man before me smiled and his unusual purple eyes brightened.

"You look a little lost."

I glanced around and realized I had no idea where I was. A paved path wound beneath under my feet. Many of the graves had carvings on them. The landscape was manicured with flowers and trees. I heard bird songs and the distinct hum of traffic in the background. There was no traffic in the dimension where I took souls to. I appeared in the center of the boneyard, standing in a nexus of realities similar to that of my house where various universes came together. My skin prickled at the seams as the different planes played over my flesh.

"Who are you?"

He stuck his hand out. "Name's Oliver. Nice to meet you. I take it you didn't realize you would end up here after you were done taking your souls in."

"No, not really. I was thinking and must've taken the wrong path."

"Happens to the best of us."

"The thinking part or taking the wrong road?"

Oliver laughed. "You have a sense of humor. Do you know how rare that is among reapers?"

"About one in ten actually know what a joke is. I'm Kerstin. It's nice to meet you, Oliver. Where am I?" I shook his hand.

"This is my own little slice of reality I like to call home."

"Not many reapers can say that they have a home. "

"Not many reapers can claim to be as beautiful as you, either."

"What a silver tongued devil you are, but I'm already spoken for. If I'm correct, there's traffic going by. Not something that'd be happening in a regular graveyard. But..." This didn't feel like any regular cemetery either. Some spirits lingered around the crypts. At first they appeared to be normal ghosts, but they vibrated on another frequency. "What kind of souls are these?"

"Ahh...you've noticed the difference. Come with me, and I'll explain."

I glanced back the way that I had come and didn't see anything following me. It wasn't very often I met another reaper who was so intriguing.

"Sure. Why not? I got time to spare."

"That's definitely something I don't hear a reaper saying. We're always on the go. No one waits for death or death waits for no one. I always get that one confused." Oliver walked toward the sounds of civilization, and I followed. As I passed a few phantasms, I noticed many had their mouths sewn shut. That wasn't something I saw every day. They watched after me with longing eyes.

"Why do they linger when you could've brought them over?"

The closer we were to the front, the heaviness of the real world settled upon me. When we passed outside of the gates, the weight of the world descended. The air was thicker to breathe as though steeped in moisture and humidity. The bird songs were different. The sky was bluer and not tainted with as much pollution. The sun sank lower revealing the sparkling stars. The heavenly bodies were in a different position than in my reality, but the constellations remained the same.

"Those who remain in the 'yard are there for punishment because of the things they've done in life."

"But we bring them to the other world to find peace. We're not their judges."

"True, but the souls here aren't human. They are vampires, werewolves, dark fairies, all types of supernatural creatures. All who are paying for their deeds by their death and their imprisonment. The rules are different when it comes to the supernatural. Even how we collect their souls."

"Is that why their mouths are sewn shut?"

We stopped in front of a house. It was old with the paint peeling and the shutters missing on a couple windows. There was a hearse parked in the driveway in front of the garage. The door was open at the side when we walked up to it.

"Hey, Abner. You around?" Oliver held the door for me.

"Thanks. Who lives here?"

"An associate of mine. You asked why the souls had their mouths sewn shut. He's the man who does that." Oliver led me through the kitchen, into the hallway where he opened the down into the basement. I followed behind him. We came to another, thicker, door. Oliver pounded on it. "Abner, it's Oliver. I have someone here who wants to meet you." He turned back to me. "Sorry. We could just pop in, but I don't want to give him a heart

61

attack. Poor guy deals with enough with some of the bodies he brings in. Never can tell when one of them is just stunned or dead."

I nodded, not really seeing or understanding the point of meeting Oliver's colleague. The door opened after a minute. The man on the other side could've been someone's grandfather. He had kind eyes and a white wispy mustache. A crisp white apron covered most of his clothing. A dark purple almost black line ringed his aura along with vibrant yellow and orange. He was very much alive, that much was plain to see. Nevertheless, I had come across people who were touched by death, and they had this same dark purple ring in their aura. This could mean they were a psychic embroiled with ghosts. Or a regular person who had an encounter with a grim reaper and might not have known it. Normally it was a very small line. His band was so thick I wondered if he was part reaper because he certainly was an agent of death.

Abner wiped his hands on his apron. A corpse laid on the metal table behind him. "Oliver, you're early. I haven't finished working yet."

"Sorry, but I ran into a colleague, and she wanted to meet you. Had some questions about some of the ghosts in the graveyard."

Abner turned his gaze on me and smiled. He stuck out his hand. "Abner Archer, Undertaker. Pleased to meet you."

"Kerstin Palmer. Nice to meet you. Undertaker? Why do you need to prep the bodies before their soul is reaped? I've never heard of that."

"You must be a different sort of harvester than Oliver."

"Harvester?" I glanced at the other reaper. "That's an odd term for reaping."

Oliver shrugged. "We do things a bit differently than what you're used to."

"Hmm." I hadn't come to this little slice of reality before to reap souls. If I had, I hadn't noticed the differences. Nothing else mattered when I was in the groove. The world passed by, and all I thought about were souls. "Different isn't a bad thing. Abner, what do you do to these corpses?"

Abner motioned me over to the table. A young man no more than fourteen or fifteen lay on the worktable. His red hair fanned out on the table. A sprinkling of freckles dappled his nose. A silver dagger protruding from his chest broke up the serene tableau. He pointed toward the weapon. "You're wondering why I haven't removed the knife."

"Yes."

"This fairy will reanimate. If that happens, it'll easily kill me and go back to doing whatever dastardly deeds it was doing before the hunters brought it to me."

"Fairy? Really?"

"Amazed yet? I take it you don't have fae in your realm?" Oliver leaned against the door.

"No. We don't. At least none I've come across. Ghosts, demons, the devil, you know the usual."

"Devil? I'd love to hear that story." Abner's mustache twitched as he laughed.

"Maybe some other time. How do you process the bodies? Harvest the souls."

"The hunters bring me the bodies, and I bring them here. It's been that way for thousands of years where undertakers process the bodies. The weapons remain in them. Then we use our tools to sew the mouth shut, trapping the soul within the body until the harvester gathers the soul and destroys the body if needed."

Abner finished sewing the fairy's mouth shut. Then he drew two coins out of a beat-up tin on the rolling tray next to him and placed them on the corpse's eyes. The energy of the soul trapped within the fairy cried out for release.

"The coins pay the way for the dead. I thought you put them in the mouth?"

Abner shrugged. "This was the way I was taught by my predecessor."

"It doesn't really matter. As long as there's a coin." Oliver walked over to the corpse and placed his lips on its. A ribbon of blue energy passed between his lips and the body. His eyes sparked purple. I caught a glimmer of his skull and the dark cloak. He flashed me a boney grin with a couple teeth missing. The body convulsed. "I'll be back. Abner can answer any more questions you might have."

Oliver winked out. I glanced around the room and noticed a curio cabinet. The things in it appeared to be a mishmash of oddities. I touched one of the glass panels. A twinge of energy passed through my fingertips.

"That's odd," Abner declared.

"What do you mean?"

"Normally, anyone that touches the cabinet is blown across the room or zapped to holy hell. Only my assistant and I are able to open it and touch the things inside."

"Not even Oliver?"

"No, but he knows better than to touch it. He's had years of experience."

"What's in here?"

Abner took out a key, unlocked it, and the cabinet doors swung open inviting me inside. The shelves were lined with all different kinds of oddities and an inch of dust. Mason jars were filled with things I'd never seen before. There were weapons and ancient books, a scroll or two in the back. One thing caught my eye. A green and black beetle the size of a half dollar sat on the shelf. I went to pick it up, but Abner grabbed my hand.

"I wouldn't do that if I were you."

"Why not?"

"It's dangerous. It'll burrow under your skin in a second and eat you up from the inside out. It was owned by an Egyptian high priest. He ended up a mummy and wreaking havoc back in the day. My predecessor dealt with him. It took her four tries to get his soul pinned down."

"All these things are trinkets you get from the dead?"

"In a way, I guess you could say that. We collect anything that might be used as a weapon or cursed. Most everything you see is dangerous. We undertakers keep them so they don't get out into the public. Sometimes we're called to an object, but it's rather rare."

"How many of you are there? Undertakers I mean?"

Abner twirled his mustache. "A couple dozen in the states. Maybe less. Around the world, I really don't know. We don't exactly stay in touch. The whole system is well…it's kind of a secret society."

"Each of you has a reaper that tends a graveyard with souls in it?"

"Yes. Is there something I can get you to drink or eat?"

He was a very nice gentleman. It sounded like a quiet life that I could deal with. "Not unless you can tell me anything about dead grim reapers and what might be killing them."

Abner leaned back against the table and rubbed his chin. "It's funny you say that. I came across something in my office that mentions something about that. It seems Oliver is going to be detained a little while longer. Let's go upstairs, and I'll put on some tea."

I followed him up into the kitchen. It seemed so odd that I'd end up here. Here was a nice man who did things that I had no idea ever existed. It always blew my mind and made me grateful that I had the ability to traverse different realms because I always learned new things. Back in the kitchen, I saw it was a regular place. There were kitchen cabinets, and the fridge. The house was larger on the inside than I saw on the outside. I heard footsteps coming toward the kitchen from the hallway behind me. There was another hallway that led into a backroom or a back porch.

"Hey, Abe, I have to get going. You got any grub for the road? I was…" the man stopped when he saw me. "Oh, sorry. I didn't realize that Abe had company."

"He went to get something in his office. I'm sure he'll be down in a second."

"It's fine. I was just on my way out. I had a job come up." The man set his cowboy hat on his head and tipped it. "Ma'am, just tell him that I left."

"And you are?" I inquired while studying the man. He was almost seven feet tall. His brown hair was pulled into a ponytail. His brown eyes were sleep laden, and his clothes disheveled. At any rate, he was cute. If I was available, I'd think about dating him.

He flashed me a quick smile and stuck out his hand. "I'm Stockton."

I shook his hand and nearly lost mine in his large grip. It was firm, and there was something different about him. I couldn't really place it. "Kerstin. Nice to meet you."

"Perhaps I'll see you around." He grabbed his coat from the chair and slipped it on before walking out the door.

Once he was gone, Abner came downstairs carrying a large leather bound book and something else wrapped up in a cloth. The undertaker set the things on the table and went to the stove to boil water and got out cups and tea.

"All I have is lemon or chamomile."

"Lemon is fine."

"I knew I'd like you. Lemon is my favorite. Do you take sugar or milk?"

"Neither, thanks. Does it normally take this long for Oliver to deliver the souls?"

"It *has* been awhile, but he'll be back soon. Sometimes he goes off for a bit. I'm sure other things come up."

I nodded and glanced around the kitchen, noticing the old fashioned dusty spice rack filled with small bottles that hadn't been used in ages. On top of the cabinets were a couple vases of brittle dried flowers that had seen better days. My thoughts turned to Than. Maybe he had gotten caught up in collecting souls like Oliver. With the beasts trolling the cemetery I wanted him to be safe. Azrael might have me focused on what was killing the other reapers, but Than was more important. I clutched the feather pendent I had on and concentrated on my dark angel. I didn't feel anything out of sorts.

"Your tea is ready."

Abner's voice drew me back to reality. "Sorry."

"It's okay. I assume you were thinking about someone special. The way you were holding that charm I take it someone you care for gave it to you."

"Yes. Very special."

He handed me the cup of tea. "I didn't realize that harvesters were allowed, or could have, relationships."

I blew the steam from the piping liquid and dunked the

bag a few times before answering. "It's rare, but we can. With our schedules, it's rather difficult because it's not like people wait for death, and we don't wait for them."

The undertaker chuckled. "This is true. The bodies the hunters bring have to be processed right away just in case something happens and they reanimate. There's always that chance." He pointed to the long scar on the side of his face.

"Did this used to be a funeral home? Do you work on regular people?"

"No. Although we could if we had to. I have my undertaker's license. There's no need for us to work on normal people. This was one of the first houses built in this little town purchased by my predecessor. I was with her when she did. Those were the days. Business hasn't slowed any, but it comes in waves."

"Wait. You were here when the house was bought? It's at least one hundred and fifty years old. How old are you?"

He sipped his tea. "Almost two hundred and fourteen in three months. Enough about me. You had asked about grim reapers. It's funny because I was going through some of the old journals and came across an entry that mentions reapers. There's something I think you might need."

He pulled the book closer and set the cloth wrapped package to the side. The leather creaked from the binding as he opened the book. Everything on the table jumped as the cover landed on the hard surface. The pages were yellowed from age, and the writing faded in a few spots. He ran his fingers lovingly over the pages. It was not written in English, but from the way he skimmed over the pages it was clear he could understand them.

"Was this passed down through your family?"

"No. It's from four undertakers ago. Olaf was his name. He was Romanian, dealt with a lot of witches. He wasn't around too long, it seems, maybe thirty years. I don't know what happened to him, but this is his journal. We all keep records of what we do and what we come across. It helps in case we happen upon something we don't know about. There's a great deal of knowledge within these pages. Normally, I wouldn't take this out of my office, but I figured I'd make an exception with you being a harvester and all. Let's see…"

I sipped my tea. It was sourer than I was used to. Undertakers were either immortal or gained some sort of longevity when they took on the job, if he had been around for over two hundred years. He didn't look more than sixty-five. "Oh, Stockton said to tell you he was leaving because a job came in, and he would see you next time."

"Thank you. We keep a back room made up for the hunters in case they need to get a night's sleep. They keep odd hours so the door's always open, and we keep the fridge stocked."

"You say we? Is there another undertaker here or someone that I should be worried about?"

"No. Sorry. My assistant. She's off running errands today. I don't know when she'll be back. Nice young girl." He looking through the journal until he was almost half way through it. "Ahh." He tapped his finger on the page. "Here's what I was looking for."

I stood up and looked over his shoulder. Besides the handwriting being barely legible it was written in some other language. "How do you know what that says? Unless you're Romanian too."

"Actually, it's Russian, and it's complicated. It comes with the job. I'm sure you have certain abilities that come with your office."

"Yes. We do."

"This is what Olaf writes…" Abner put on his glasses "'Today had a very unusual case come into the shop. At first, I thought nothing about it and went back to baking the bread as the woman looked over our goods. After a moment, she collapsed on the floor. I had Hans take her into the back and try to rouse her with some water. However, she did not awake right away and called for me. I sat next to her, and she shoved something into my arms and insisted I keep it safe. Blackness traveled along her veins into her face. Her bright blue eyes were dimming. When I peeled the shirt away from her neck, jagged claw marks dug deep into her shoulder. I tried to help her, but she said there was no helping death. She was a harvester. I'd never known them to be hurt or even to die. How does one kill death when they're already dead?

"'What did this to you?' I asked."

"'Went to the wrong place. I was attacked by his guard dogs. Didn't know he was still around. We were told…I thought…'"

"'She swooned in my arms and was gone. I didn't know what she meant about going to the wrong place. I laid her on the table and examined her wound further. She'd been gored by a rather large canine. The claw pattern was different than a werewolf. I doubted those beasts would attempt an attack on a harvester. The poison originated from these scratches. They went from her shoulder down the front of her chest stopping just above her waist. When I poked at them, something moved within her flesh. I grabbed a large pair of tongs and withdrew a curved claw similar to a lion's.'"

I felt the blood drain from my face and replaced with ice as he read those words. It brought me back to the beast that had gotten me. This thing that attacked the other reaper in the past sounded like the creatures that stalked the graveyard now.

"'It wasn't very soon after she expired her body withered away, leaving behind a few loose black feathers. I told my harvester what happened, but he had no explanation.'" Abner closed the book and rested his glasses on top of it. He took the package and was about to unwrap it when a large crash interrupted us. We both jumped up and turned to investigate. Lying on the stone steps halfway through the backdoor was a large dark shape slumped over the window of the door. A few of the glass pieces scrunched under my boots. Blood stained the glass and ran down the bottom of the door. I lifted him up and dragged him through the rest of the window. Oliver screamed as I turned him over.

"Oliver, what happened?" Abner asked.

He opened his mouth to talk, but nothing came out. His face twisted in an expression of pain. His unique purple eyes were wide with terror. Claw marks scoured his left shoulder down his chest. They resembled the ones the paramedics had after they were attacked in my driveway. Already the black vines of poison spread through his veins. Oliver had a few minutes at most.

Azrael was the only one who could heal him.

"Is he going to be okay?" Abner asked.

"He doesn't have a lot of time. I hope you don't mind company." I glanced at Abner. I closed my eyes and shifted everything I was so I basked in the coldness of death. All I heard were the celestial winds until even those quieted.

"Azrael." My call traveled through the vastness of space. It didn't matter where I was, he would find me. I opened my eyes. Abner was pale. His eyes were wide as though someone had walked over his grave. My wings flexed them. They brushed the edges of the walls. I glanced at my hands and saw they were flesh.

"What are you really?" Abner whispered.

A frigid blast sliced through the kitchen, lifting the heavy cover of the book he brought down and knocking off his glasses. Azrael stood before us with a rift sealing behind him. A few stars winked out in the tear. Abner gasped and fell back on his ass, scrambling to get away.

"What is it, Kerstin?" Azrael asked. "Did you find the beast yet?"

Oliver convulsed and black foam spewed from his mouth. His eyes rolled back in his head. His flesh turned ashen while the blackness of the poison branched through his veins. I glanced at my boss. "He was attacked by one of those things. You have to heal him. He knows what they look like."

Azrael knelt by Oliver and placed his hand on his head. He shivered and rooted around in one of the gouges left by the animal. My boss pulled out a four-inch curved claw that belonged more on a dinosaur than it did some kind of canine or an enormous cat. He dropped it to the floor and shot me a look. "Don't touch it. There's still poison on it."

Oliver's wound began to heal. The darkness in his veins receded, and his eyes cleared. He gasped and tried to get up, but I held him down. "Take a minute. Abner, would you make some more tea please?"

The undertaker got up slowly and backed toward the cupboard. Oliver's gaze settled on Azrael. As I held him, I felt Oliver quaking.

"Are you well enough to tell us what happened, Oliver?" Azrael asked.

"Y-you know my n-name?" Oliver stammered.

Our boss chuckled. "Of course I do. Being the harvester for an undertaker is an esteemed position. Very few can do it. Who do you think picked you for the job?"

He gazed at me with astonishment. He touched his chest. "I'm alive."

The whistle of the tea kettle sounded until Abner pulled it

off the stove. Oliver stood up and paced the kitchen. I sat back at the table and sipped the tea. Abner handed a cup to Oliver and one to Azrael, trying to avoid touching him. He sat across from me. Oliver continued to wear a path into the floor.

"I went to into the graveyard to deliver the soul of the fairy. He went into the fog to go wherever his kind goes. I turned to come back when I saw a blur of darkness. I thought it might be a shadow of a soul lost and wandering. I've seen them before, so I didn't think much of it and went to help it. As I approached it, I realized it wasn't a spirit. It morphed into something that wasn't quite a dog or a feline."

It followed me.

"Did it speak to you?"

"I didn't hear it talk, but it laughed. It was more of a human laugh mixed with a growl. I backed away, but it leapt at me. The pain of the claws paralyzed me. I wasn't sure I was going to be able to get out of there alive. I just focused on here. Sir, what was that thing?" He looked at Azrael.

Azrael tapped his finger on the tea cup before setting it down on the counter. "I don't know. That's why I have Kerstin looking into it."

"I've heard rumors about something stalking the cemetery. How could something get into the graveyard unless it slipped between the cracks? All the souls within the graveyard are bound by the iron fence that surrounds the place. Their remains are bound to the ground. They can't move until they've completed their penance."

"Kerstin, do you know what the creature is?" Oliver tried to drink his tea, but his hand shook. Liquid sloshed over the sides of the cup and onto the floor. Azrael grabbed the cup from him and guided him to sit down at the table.

"I don't know what it is. That's what I was telling Abner. He said he discovered something in his book. An account of a reaper being hurt by something similar. It gouged her, and then she died. She said something about being in the wrong place, and she thought he was gone. Azrael, have any reapers disappeared over the years?"

A deep line of worry appeared across Azrael's pale forehead. He raked his hands through his hair pulling it from the ponytail. The dark tendrils fell over his shoulders. It made him look more human. "It happens on occasion. One will get lost here and there. A few move on to other things or higher realms, depending on what they get called to do. I only rule over the dead and nothing else. I wouldn't say more than a handful. Why?"

"What if the vanishing reapers is more than you think? No offense, but you just don't notice everything because you're so scattered all the time. You take time off to be with Brenna. What if more get lost than you know? There are cracks in all the realities. What if this is happening in all worlds where there is death. Do you even know how many reapers serve you?"

"I don't like your tone, Kerstin," Azrael growled.

"I don't mean any disrespect. I'm just thinking."

"What if there are more disappearances than you know?" Oliver asked.

"I've never heard of attacks like this before."

"This big shadow animal that mauled Oliver. I've seen it, too. It attacked some local campers behind my house and then killed two paramedics. It told me that next time it saw me I'd have to make the right choice. It had claws the size of my hand. What if this big one is the pack leader? At first I thought maybe it was a hellhound working with Mastema. But it didn't feel like him."

"Is he still after you?" Azrael sipped at his tea.

"He pops into my mind once in a while. He tried to seduce me into using the boon he granted me."

"Anything else?" Azrael inquired.

"He can reach through the cracks and touch me." I wasn't about to tell my boss how the devil made me feel. How deep down I craved his touches. I fought it with all my reaper will, but he was the devil. One touch by him set my insides quivering. It was lust and nothing more. But damn.

"He shouldn't be able to do that." Azrael grimaced at the tea.

"You converse with the devil? How can you when he's fallen into hell?" Abner looked between me and my boss.

"It's a long story."

"My brother is more cunning than you realize, Undertaker. It's best not to invite him here by talking about him. Kerstin, we will deal with this later."

"He says he'll tell me what's going on if I ask him so that he won't be in my debt anymore."

"What did you tell him?" Oliver appeared completely recovered. Even the tears in his suit had been repaired.

"I keep telling him no. Did you expect I would cave? I don't have a burning desire to be attached to him more than I already am. Because you know that's what he wants. It was bad enough last year with the serial killer. I really don't want to have a repeat of it. Back on topic, any idea what these shadow beasts are? Maybe they could be soul hunters, but see the reapers as more powerful prey?" I suggested.

"A few other things have been going on," Oliver admitted.

"What do you mean?" Azrael inquired.

"I've noticed the veils between some of the worlds are thinner. The harmonics are off. The universal songs are airy, like the player isn't pursing his lips just right. I don't know how else to explain it. The dead are feistier like they know something's coming. Abe, remember that one who came in a month or so again. A hunter brought her in. We had a hard time classifying her."

"Yes. She looked like an ordinary person. When you tried to find her soul, there wasn't anything there. Oliver removed the stake. She revived and was terrified. She insisted she had gotten lost and wandered through the wrong doorway. What was her name… Rohe something?"

"I took her into the cemetery. She said that she was lost. A bad burn scar deformed the right side, and the other half was fine. She had black hair and dark eyes. I tried to talk to find out more about her, but she strolled off into the graveyard and disappeared."

"You mean she went into the fog," Azrael stated.

"No. I mean she walked among the gravestones as if she was right at home, and then disappeared. The hunter who brought her in said the only way he could subdue her was by staking her, and even that was difficult. She was alive but immobile."

Azrael sighed. By his expression, I knew he had an inkling of what might be going on. "Thank you for the information. If you hear anything unusual from the other harvesters please let me know. Kerstin, I have to look into something. Has Than returned yet?"

"No, he hasn't come back yet. I'm beginning to worry about him."

"I'm sure he'll turn up."

In his usual fashion, he disappeared. I glanced back to Oliver and Abner. "He does that."

"I didn't realize you knew the boss personally," Oliver said with a bit of wonder in his voice.

"Please. Dealing with him at times is like talking to a brick wall. He goes poof and doesn't hear what I have to say. This isn't the first time." I rubbed my eyes, feeling a headache form between them. It was either this reality getting to me or all of the information I'd taken in. Maybe it was dealing with the boss. Sometimes I wish he'd tell me what he thought was going on or not get off track like when he brought Mastema up. I didn't need to be reminded about him. "Abner, we didn't scare you too badly, did we? For a moment, it looked like you might have a heart attack when Azrael appeared."

The undertaker laughed. "No. But I never thought you'd be so beautiful. I've only seen Oliver and how he deals with the souls. I had no idea you were angels, too."

"Did I forget to mention that, old man?" Oliver clapped him on the back.

It would have been good to stay and talk with them. I am sure there was much more I could learn. I sighed. I had obligations at home. Raj and Morana would be wondering where I was. "Oliver. Abner. It was nice to meet you. I'm glad that you're both okay, but I need to be heading back. I have things to take care of in my own world. As you know, not doing what the boss wants can get one in trouble. I have to figure out exactly what these things are and what is going on. Oliver, can you walk me back to the graveyard?"

"Of course." Oliver started toward the door when Abner grabbed my arm.

"Don't forget this. It might help." He held out the bound bundle he had set on the table. "Also keep this." He pressed another thing wrapped in cloth into my hand. I opened it to find the talon Azrael removed from Oliver.

"You don't even know what it is. Are you sure? Maybe you should keep this with your collection." I held it back to him.

He closed the package, placed his hand over mine, and squeezed. "I have a feeling it'll help you. Don't know why, but you coming here is not a coincidence. The talon belongs with you."

I gave him a quick hug. I slipped the wrapped claw into my jeans pocket. I had too many strange things happen to me over the years never to think anything was a coincidence. The universe provided when it needed to. "Thank you."

"Come again soon. I'll make some more tea." Abner mustache tickled when pressed his lips to my cheek.

"Sounds good."

I followed Oliver out of the door and back down the street. As I was leaving, I saw another car pull into the driveway with a woman driving. "That's Abner's assistant," Oliver volunteered.

We arrived at the front gates for the cemetery. They were large, wrought iron with the name of the boneyard scrolled in an arch over the entrance. Every time I tried to read the name, it blurred out of focus. The letters kept rearranging themselves. The whole place was surrounded by the fence. Spirits lingered close to the enclosure, but they never hung on the bars the way I had seen other spirits do.

"Oliver, what's with the name of the cemetery? It's going to give me a migraine if I look at it too much longer."

Oliver passed through the locked gates. He chuckled. "I wasn't sure if you noticed that. It confuses the humans, so whenever they think of wanting to bury anyone here then they can't remember the name because it's different all the time."

Understandable. "What about her?" I gestured toward a woman walking her dog inside the boneyard. "Isn't it dangerous to the public to be in here?"

Oliver glanced over his shoulder. "There's a couple of side gates so people can walk their dogs or picnic in here if they want to. I was partial to the days when humans would come to a cemetery and enjoy the day when there were more gardens. That is why there are a lot of flowers and trees here. Over the hill is a pond where many like to go. The other gates close at nightfall. The whole place is spelled so that people have a compulsion to leave. Iron bars run underneath where the gates are so nothing can get out even during the day."

It all sounded logical. This was his reality, so I had no idea of the rules here unless I stayed long enough to orient myself to it. Every place was different. I shook my head and walked through the gates. The iron tickled a little. This place had more of a slightly overgrown garden look to it. There were large open spaces with plenty of trees and flowers mixed among the stones and crypts. However, it held nothing to the serenity of my graveyard. The phantasms we passed had their mouth's sewn shut. I wasn't sure how I felt about that, but this wasn't my reality to make judgments on. Two spirits waited for me who were too scared to go into the graveyard alone. I didn't blame them. I had to be extra careful now.

We strolled to the middle. It stretched for an eternity in every direction. The sounds of traffic had dissipated, and the bird songs were faint.

"I'm sorry this happened. You wouldn't have been attacked if I showed up."

"Who knows? Meeting you has been interesting. Whatever is hunting reapers has to be powerful to control this pack running loose. It would make sense they are all being controlled by someone. Personally, I think it's the devil, but Azrael ruled that out. Who does that leave?"

"I don't know what it is, but what you said makes sense. Someone has to be controlling it—them. But I don't know anyone who has that kind of power and would want to hurt reapers. We're not doing any harm. We help souls."

"True, but we're also angels. Look, I don't know the answer any more than you do. I hope you figure it out. I'll be more careful next time I see a rogue shadow in the graveyard. It was nice to meet you. Please visit again, or if you need help don't hesitate to ask."

"Thanks, Oliver. Same to you. I'll be more than happy to assist with something if you need it. By the way, how do I get out of here?"

"Just follow the path to your left."

"Thanks." I slipped the package Abner gave me into a pocket deep inside of my robe so I wouldn't lose it. *Oliver said, it has to be a powerful being to control the shadow creature that came to my doorstep. But who?* Azrael set me to the task of discovering the culprit.

One day, I really hoped I wouldn't be the bait.

CHAPTER SEVEN

I walked the paths of the cemetery. Once I was out of Oliver's boneyard, I took the time to notice the tombstones. Massive sculptures of half shorn trees and a roll top desk marked a grave. Another was a weeping angel learning over a stone. Some were very simple. A tiny headstone with a lamb or a cherub. Others were large slate stones chipping away even in the eternity of this place. The lesson to be learned from this was that nothing was impossible here. In all my years as a reaper, I'd never taken the time to notice the differences in the graveyards tended by other reapers. I should have paid more attention. It made me heartsick. We were supposed to care for the dead, and I hadn't been doing my duty to the fullest. I stopped and ran a hand over one of the tombstones.

A shadow darted between one of the stones. I summoned the scythe to my hand. I waited. The shadow stood in the isle and blocking my path. Another blur caught my attention to my right. Maybe this was another reaper who needed assistance. I looked over and didn't see the shadow any more. When I turned back, the original shadow remained in the distance. My heartbeat quickened. I glanced to the left and saw my part of the cemetery. I was close to home and reuniting with Than. If this was another reaper, then I had an obligation to help my fellow dark angel.

The human part of me said to forget it and save my own skin. But I was more reaper than human these days. No matter what, I was going to go check it out. I kept my scythe ready to swipe at anything that came out after me. The farther I walked, the farther away the dark figure got. There seemed no end as to how far I had to get in order to reach the shadow. Grave markers grew older. A tingling sensation passed over me each time I went into a different realm. The atmosphere grew heavier. After walking for an unknown amount of time the world stopped moving. I got within a few feet of the dark shadows and it solidified into a robed figure. A long hood draped over its face. It guarded the entrance to the cemetery beyond. Behind the figure green grass faded into a flat barren landscape.

"Who are you?" I held the scythe inches from the being's throat.

"A friend."

"If you're a friend, then why not show me your face?"

"To show you my face would only hasten my doom. Put your scythe away. I shall not hurt you."

I gripped the weapon and looked around the graveyard. I didn't see anything looming in the graves' shadows. "If it's all the same to you, I'll keep it handy just in case you decide to send one of those beasts to tear my throat out."

"I'm not the one sending out the hounds."

"Then who is?" I asked. "You know, I take it."

"I know who sends out the dogs to gather reapers. But it's not just reapers that the hounds collect. They take people, too. Anyone who can give him souls to empower the well. Just like your friend."

I heard the words, and my heart sank. "Than."

"No. Not the other reaper. The one who now lies an empty shell in a hospital."

Empty shell. I ran through all the people I knew. "You mean Nick."

"Yes. His soul lingers in the well untouched by the ancient one, but I don't know for how much longer."

"Are you talking about Mastema? Do you work for the devil? Are you the spirit who came to me in the run-down house?"

"No. I do not work for the fallen one. To even suggest it sickens me. But that does not mean my master hasn't been working with him. The one who came to you has already been punished and gave her life so that she could warn you. Just as I am doing."

"Who are you? Who is your master?"

A long eerie howl broke the silence. The being looked behind into the wasteland and turned back toward me. "He knows that something's amiss. He's sent out the hounds. I must go. If I'm found with you, then I'll be thrown into the well."

"Wait! How do I know what's going on? How do I save the other reapers? How do I save Nick? What the hell is going on?"

"Seek your answers in the tombs." The being vanished.

Tombs? There were millions, maybe billions of tombs on this plane.

It was all one big graveyard. *How and where am I supposed to start looking?* I didn't have all the time in the world. She hadn't mentioned Than. Hopefully, he was safe. She had mentioned Nick. He'd been the cameraman with us at Death's Dance who originally didn't believe in ghosts. Nick made a deal with Sariel to film everything. The last time I had seen Nick was when the serial killer was using psychics and their souls to fuel the devil's return to this plane. Souls were a raw source of power. If they could fuel the opening of a dimensional portal, they could help bring about the apocalypse. Something else about what that messenger said nagged at me.

A howl erupted again. Several shapes sprinted toward me from the desert. I opened my wings and willed myself back to my part of the cemetery. The click of the beasts' claws scraped the paved paths right behind me. *I have to get to the oak tree. It's a portal I can use to get back to my world.* They remained on my heels, but I made it to the tree. The protective branches loomed over me. Their shadows brought me a moment of peace so I could catch my breath. Panting sounded in my ear. I gazed around and saw the creatures. Three of them. The size of Great Danes, but much meaner. Their pointed ears were alert. Black coats the color of shiny onyx gleamed in the obscured light. Their eyes were black ringed with gold. The bigger one of the three glanced at the other two and gestured with his head for them to start circling me. He stared at me with intelligence. They meant business. *What did the figure say to me?* They hunt down souls and reapers to bring them back to a well. Since reapers were angels they would be a powerful addition to anyone's arsenal. A small part of the cosmos, and if you killed one it was like killing a star and watching it burst. Meaning everyone felt the absence of that light.

The other two encircled the tree getting closer. I stared at the lead hound. The bark underneath my hand grew softer. I slipped into the tree and left that world behind. My heart throttled against my chest. I'd come to being one of the reapers I was searching for. Sometimes tempting fate was not a good idea. I calmed myself and noticed I had arrived at the graveyard on my property. The sun had broken over the horizon.

Sarah and the other spirits lingered in the boneyard. Morana was nowhere to be found. "You've returned. I was worried you would not. It's been a long time since you left. Shadows have patrolled the grounds looking for you. And then there were others." She offered me her hand to get up.

I took it and grabbed a stone nearest me to steady myself. "Do you know what they looked like or what they were here for? What happened to Morana? Have you seen Than?"

"No, I haven't seen Than. Morana went into the house after you left. I saw men inside. I entered. I hope you don't mind, but I needed to check on the boy I saw you with. I think they're both scared, but..." She wrapped her hands into the folds of her skirt. Her face had paled even more for a dead woman.

"Sarah, what's the matter? You can tell me anything. I'm not going to send you to the other side for telling me what you think's best for this place. You've been protecting it all this time. Tell me what's on your mind."

"You've been gone for four days. I've been watching the young man and the girl. I don't know. They don't have the feel of the dead. I can't explain it. You have to look—"

"Hey, Kerstin!"

I turned. Angela stood by the house with bags in her hands and a huge smile on her face. She dropped the luggage and ran at me. She embraced me. The impact of her body brought me all the way back into the physical world. My robe melted away revealing the jeans and T-shirt that I had on. "Why are you here? I thought you were in school."

Angela stepped back. "You said I could come anytime. So here I am."

"What about school?"

She rolled her eyes. "I'm on break. I didn't want to go home and deal with my mother. She's such a bitch. I hope you don't mind me being here."

"No. It's just a surprise. Come on inside, and I'll get a room ready for you."

Angela's smile returned. "What's up with the woman you were talking to? She seems sad."

I glanced back at Sarah. Her hands were wound tight into her skirt. "I'll come back out later, and we can finish our conversation."

The ghost nodded and drifted away, vanishing into mist and then nothingness.

"This is a wild place. There's so much energy. It's like you have the Northern Lights all the time. How do you deal with it without making you sick?"

"You get used to it." We got to the back door. Angela knew I was a gifted psychic and that Than was a grim reaper, but that was all. She had no idea about my true identity. I wasn't about to tell her even if she was supposed to be my student. Her aura appeared clouded. She was trying to hide something from me.

I set her bags on the floor and closed the door. I grabbed a couple bottles of water from the fridge and handed one to her. The fridge was empty. Morana and Raj must have eaten me out of house and home. A cold chill rushed by me. Morana stood in the doorway between the kitchen and the living room.

She gazed at me with that blank expression. Her appearance was gray. The wound around her throat was livid and bleeding. White things curled around the edge of her gash. Her eyes were more sunken in. Maybe it was because she had eaten. Maybe it was because she was here with me in the nexus. I didn't want Angela to see her like that.

"What do you see?".

If she couldn't see Morana, then the little girl was good at hiding. "Nothing, it's been a long day. How's school going?"

Angela rubbed her hands over her arm and shivered. "It's okay. Not much to write home about." She glanced away and looked back at me.

"What's really going on?"

Angela fiddled with the water bottle. She twisted the cap off and shot it across the room. "Damnit. Am I that transparent?"

I retrieved the cap and set it on the counter. "We've gotten to know one another. I like to think we have a good relationship, that you'd be truthful with me. I'm not your mother, so I'm not going to judge. What's the real reason you left school and came here?" I hated to sound harsh, but I was in no mood. If she was here, she was in danger.

"You're such a good psychic, why don't you figure it out?" she snapped.

"You know it doesn't work that way." If I truly wanted, I could read her mind or touch her soul. I would never violate her that way. It was one thing to delve into her future, it was another to be a reaper and rape her soul.

"You're different."

"And you're avoiding my question."

"No, I'm serious. Your energy's changed. It's cooler. That dark line in your aura's almost blocking out the light. Is everything okay?"

"Stop changing the subject. You showed up on my doorstep, so don't try and put one over on me." I heard the severity of my tone, but there was nothing I could do to stop the words from coming out. I didn't care if she sensed the difference in me or not, I had more to think about than a willful teenager.

"Sorry. I didn't think it was such an imposition." Angela growled, but something had her spooked. She went to her bags.

"Angela, what happened?" I grabbed her arm.

Her eyes brimmed with tears ready to spill over. Her arm was shaking. She threw her arms around me and sobbed. I hugged her and rubbed her back until she calmed down. I separated her from me and made some tea. It took a few more minutes for her to become coherent. Morana lingered in the living room listening. Her presence disturbed me. Her energy raked over my soul with wet fingers. There was a silence in her I hadn't noticed before. It came from being around too long, a wisdom of ages that she shouldn't possess. Maybe I was reading her wrong, and she was only curious about Angela. Morana probably sensed the darkness that lingered around Angela because of the touch of death within her. Than and I had intervened and freed her from a leech attached to her aura. It had wanted to suck the life out of Angela and eventually possess her if it had the chance. Her mother didn't believe in psychics. These past few months had been interesting, trying to convince her to let me teach Angela how to harness her abilities.

"Are you listening?"

I tore my gaze away from Morana. "Sorry. I was just thinking. There's been a lot going on lately. What did you say?"

Her eyes were red and puffy. "I said something's trying to kill me."

"Kill you? Sweetie, you're powerful enough to know there isn't anything that can really hurt you. You know how to keep the bad ones away. If you were in crazy trouble all you have to do is call out for Than, and he'll come, and—"

"I did. I called for him, and he didn't come."

"Wait! What? When? He didn't come?" My heart dropped.

Shit. "Okay. Start from the beginning. Tell me what happened."

Angela pushed her hair back out of her eyes. "I was walking back from the library across campus. It was dark out. The library is haunted, but the ghosts leave me alone or I ignore them. On the way home, they hung back. Even my guides were absent. I tried to sense what was going on. Something big and mean followed me. It was bigger than a lion. I started to run and made it into a part of the park. It had me trapped. It smiled. I smelled the putrid breath. It jumped after me. I called out to Than. I figured he'd sense my fear or something. I don't know how it works. I never called on him before."

"How did you get away?"

"I ran away back toward the library. It was there. It looked like an enormous wolf or a lion or something in between. Its eyes were orangish red and yellow. The hiss of acid hit the pavement when it drooled. It wasn't normal. It didn't belong in this reality. It had me cornered. I knew once it opened its mouth it would kill me. It swiped at me. It knocked me to the ground. He stood over me, so I could smell its rancid breath, and it laughed."

It had gone after her to taunt me. "It was shadow and mass at the same time."

"How did you know?"

"I'll tell you later. Please finish." I sipped my tea and stared at Morana. Another cold breeze drifted by me. Raj stood next to Morana. His skin was sallow, as though he was rotting from the inside.

"He wrapped his jaws around my throat. I waited to die. I called to Than again, but he didn't come. He stopped, right before he was going to kill me. The monster argued with it. Something told me the monster wasn't a demon or a hellhound. It released me and said: 'I see you. I have a taste for you. I'll come back once this is over." It left me. I glimpsed the one it was arguing with. It was in a long black cloak, and a hood covered its face. I tried to get a read on it, but I couldn't. They disappeared. I ran back to my dorm and called you, but you didn't answer. I didn't know what else to do. I packed and got on a bus, then a train, and a cab to get here. That was two days ago."

The beast had a master who had shown himself. At least I knew someone pulling its strings. Although who that was remained to be seen. *It has to be Mastema. He'd be the only one who wants souls.* I reached across the table and squeezed her hand. Angela had been dragged into this because of me.

I had a couple of calls to make.

"I'm glad you came here. It was the right thing to do. I-I've seen this beast before. It killed a camper in the woods to get my attention and the EMTs that were here. Look, Angela, there's more to me than you know. I don't know where to begin to explain things. I—" The phone in the kitchen rang. I tried to ignore it, but it kept on ringing.

"It's okay. We can talk about this more when you get off the phone." Angela sipped her tea.

I grabbed it on the fourth ring. "Hello!"

"Kerstin, thank God. You gotta help me!"

Her voice was familiar, but I hadn't heard it in a while. "Doni?"

"Yeah. Please you gotta help me."

"What's going on?" I asked her.

"It's here. It's coming for me. Please. Do something. It's outside on the porch. I thought it was a coyote, but then it talked. I don't know what to do."

"Wait. What's outside?"

"They're all black. They look like wolves or something, I

don't know. Evil and darkness, it's all I can sense around them. What do I do?" Doni whimpered.

I pictured her hunkered down somewhere that she could barely see out, peeking out of the window, but they had not gotten into the house yet. I heard a crash on the other end of the phone. I focused on her, and I felt the tug of her horrified soul as it pulsated like a beacon in the night with fear. I glanced at Angela. If I disappeared, I'd have to explain it all to Angela and reveal what I was. If I didn't go, Doni could die. If I did go, she could die anyway, and I could end up being caught in the clutches of those beasts. It was the only way to save her, and I owed her one. "Find some place to hide until I can get there. Do you understand?"

"How…"

"Just do as I say. Run. Into your basement. Wherever you can go where they're not going to get you."

"Okay."

I glanced at Angela one last time and saw the concern and the wonder in her eyes. My wings opened, and I donned my reaper attire. The scythe handle was in my hand without me even thinking about it. Fear replaced the wonder as she saw my skeletal form and felt the force of my power. A scream broke her lips. A small twinge of regret hit my heart for her learning the truth. However, I was gone before I heard the rest of the shriek. I was focused on Doni, the other psychic who had helped on the reunion show for Spirit Seekers. If I could get Nick's soul back from the well, whatever that was, then she could live happily ever after with him.

Outside Doni's house, the sliding door window was broken inward. It opened from the porch and into the living room. A shadow moved inside. I held my breath and tightened my grip on the scythe. I stepped through the broken window. The tendrils of fabric on my cloak undulated before me sensing the environment. A few steps in I noticed the television set on my left nestled in an entertainment center, to the right was the couch. My weight didn't break the glass because I was insubstantial to the physical world, but I had a feeling that these hounds would see me anyway. If they roamed the land of the dead and could hurt reapers, then they were part of the dead.

A growl rumbled behind me. One of the creature's reflection showed in the television set. Its teeth were bared, and its eyes burned gold and black. Its weight cracked the glass splinters it walked on, leaving bloody footprints. The energy about it, was neither alive nor dead. Black fur covered its short and sleek muscled frame. Its ears were alert and pointed. The teeth were white, but its breath was putrid. The claws were an inch long, nothing like the one Abner had given me.

Doni was somewhere. First I needed to go through this one. "You want me? Come and get me."

Those intelligent eyes widened. With one graceful leap, it came at me. I waited as long as I could and dodged out of the way. It landed on the sofa. It clawed at the cushions tearing out the foam stuffing. It jumped at me once more, but I rolled out of the way. I stood with the dining table at my back. The creature paced, assessing the situation. Another growl echoed in the house. Then I heard a scream. I glanced over my shoulder and saw another pair of golden eyes glowering at me from the steps through the railing. Upstairs something banged against a door. The third member of the pack was trying to get at Doni. The creature in the stairwell stood up on its hind legs and leaned over the rail. They yipped at one another, communicating a message I didn't understand.

Behind me were the table and then a small wall with a

window that went into the kitchen. The one on the stairs growled again. I tried to keep my eyes on both of them. The one on the stairs curled his claws around the railing. The hound in the living room barked once more. I caught movement out of the corner of my eye just as the creature in the living room jumped. I swung the scythe and caught it diagonally through its ribcage. Blood sprayed the walls, painting it in uneven streaks. Something heavy landed on my back, knocking me down. I lost my grip on scythe. It landed out of my grasp on the carpet. The hound on my back was heavy so I could barely move. Its hot breath blasted against my back. I worked my hand free and dug it into the folds of my robe. My fingers brushed against something sharp. My hands held the hilt.

The hound on top of me yelped in pain and jumped off me. The pungent stench of burnt flesh filled the room. It gave me enough time to pull out the weapon and roll over. Scorch marks branded its muzzle and along its sides and legs where it had come into contact with the tendrils of my robe. One wisp had blinded his right eye. It rushed at me, but I dashed out of the way, slicing at it with the dagger I had pulled from my robe. I scratched its flank. It turned around and swiped at me with its claws. I stayed far enough away from those.

Doni screamed again upstairs. The pounding continued. The hound was between me and the scythe. All I had was the dagger Brenna gave me. It was old and had power to it, but I didn't know how to call upon that power. It was the power of the dead, but the blade could only do so much damage to the creature before me.

It moved around the table to guard the staircase, but keeping out of reach of my scythe. I moved to the other side. It didn't want me to get up there and save Doni. I had to find a way up there. I spied a vase of half dead gardenias on the bookcase behind me. I grabbed it and threw it into the kitchen. The beast looked at me and then into the kitchen. It moved. I jumped on the back of the beast and thrust the dagger into its neck. It yelped and collapsed on the kitchen floor. I grabbed my scythe and raced upstairs. The bedroom door was broken off the hinges and lay in pieces on the carpet. The leader of the pack was scratching at the other door in the room.

"Leave her alone."

The pack master confronted me.

"Kerstin," Doni called out from the bathroom.

"Stay calm, Doni. Don't come out."

I swiped at the creature with the scythe. The blood from the other one stained the blade. "Unless you want to meet the same fate as the two below, then I'd turn your tail and go back to your master. Tell him that going after my friends isn't a good idea. Do you understand?"

Its eyes flickered to my weapon. Its ears laid back on its head. It scraped the carpet with its claws before looking back at the door, sizing up the situation. It bared its teeth showing me its fangs. Then it lowered its head, nodding. It snapped at my blade and evaporated. I reached out my senses, and I didn't feel its presence. Once I was satisfied, I set the scythe against the wall. I opened the door and knowing that Doni might not be able to handle what she would see. I didn't care that I was breaking the cardinal rule about being a reaper and revealing myself to a living, breathing human. It was one thing to appear on camera because half of the population wasn't going to accept it anyway. Some of the other half would assume they were looking at a dark blur or a shadow person. Than and I had done it before, but we were playing with the public. Sometimes you had to have a little fun and mess with the ghost hunters.

"Doni, it's Kerstin. I need you to stay calm. I'm going to open the door. The beast is gone. Okay?"

"Okay," her voice cracked.

I slipped inside. Doni was hunched down in the bathtub, staring at me through the hazy plastic shower curtain. I pushed the curtain back.

"Please don't kill me. Shit!" She broke into unintelligible sobs.

I sat down on the side of the tub and moved the hood off revealing my true face. I touched her shoulder.

"Kerstin?"

"It's me. You don't have to be afraid. I'm not going to hurt you." I reached for her again and saw that my hand were still bones. She scurried further into the other side of the tub. I quickly vanished the visage. I tried to make her feel calm. The quicker I reassured her, the faster I could get back to Angela. Leaving her alone in the house with the other two ghosts didn't make me feel comfortable. Than not responding to her call worried me more.

Fear still lit her eyes. "It's gone. You got rid of it?"

"It's gone. Two others downstairs are dead. You're going to have to come with me, so I can keep you safe. Will you come with me?" I held out my hand to her.

She stood up slowly and took my hand. Her flesh was warm. She was alive, and I was not; well partially alive, but in this guise I was in control of death. There were things I was doing with my power I had never truly done before. This was one of them. Doni stepped out of the tub. I snapped my fingers of my free hand, and the scythe was in my grasp. I held her to me and spread my wings. I slipped between the worlds, moving so quickly that it must have stolen the breath from Doni's lungs. I arrived back in the kitchen. Angela remained at the kitchen table. Her tea was gone, and she had pulled over mine.

"You're back," Angela said.

"I am. Doni, are you okay?" I looked at the other woman and saw she was ashen.

Morana and Raj lingered in the doorway. I steered Doni over to the kitchen table and sat her down. I reheated the water and grabbed two more cups. This time I also pulled out the vodka and set that on the table, too. Doni grabbed the bottle and took a long swig. Her hands shook as she tried to set it down. Angela reached over and settled her hand. She seemed to be taking this a whole lot better than Doni was. The shriek of the tea kettle whistle broke the silence. I filled the cups with the hot water. I vanished my robe and the scythe. When I did, I remembered my dagger was still stuck in the neck of the hound. I had to go back and get it.

"I'll be right back. I left something at your house. You'll be safe here for now. Just stay inside. I'll be just a minute." I disappeared and reappeared at Doni's. Instead of the bodies of the creatures I had left behind, I saw piles of dust and bone. I'd only been gone five minutes. There wasn't much left of the first one. The blood that had splattered the walls was now streaks of ash.

The other's body in the kitchen was dried up and shriveled. Bits and pieces of what appeared to be bandages were wrapped around the hound. Underneath those bandages I saw leathery skin and bone as if it was a mummy. I pulled the dagger out of the remains. A dried beetle fell out of the beast. It was metallic green and black like the one that I had seen in Abner's Wunderkammer. He had said the beetles were scarab's and had been used by Egyptian priests. I examined the hound again and saw the bandages. *Son of a bitch.* I willed myself back to the house. The two women remained in the kitchen. The bottle of vodka was half gone.

"Are you going to tell me what the hell is going on?" Doni stared at me half slurring her words.

"We both deserve an explanation." Angela crossed her arms over her chest.

"Yes, there's a lot of explaining to do. You already know that Than's a grim reaper. I'm one, too. The images you captured on video at Death's Dance were the both of us. The serial killer killing all those psychics was after me. He wanted to free the devil from hell. I was actually killed at Death's Dance when Jackson was. However, I was given the choice to come back as a grim reaper. So I took it. Than is my soul mate. We've been together for hundreds of years. At the end of the convention last year, I was kidnapped and then killed again. It wasn't food poisoning. My boss, well he's the head Archangel of death and reinstated me as a grim reaper and —a human. That bit is a little more complicated. Things have been going fine, until well…until I had a spirit come to me and tell me that the grim reaper ferrying her to the other side was attacked. I went to investigate and discovered those beasts. They are focusing on me and people I know. It went after Angela. It came after you. Any questions?"

Doni shook her head. "I always thought there was something different about you. So…" she traced her fingers around the rim of her cup. "Are you going to kill us?"

"Of course not. I haven't killed anyone. Human any way. Grim reapers have a bad rap. People think that we murder and claim souls, but we bring peace to those that want it. We move through realities, universes and anywhere our list brings us."

"How can you be alive and doing readings, writing books, if

you're off collecting souls?" Angela asked.

"I'm not on active duty. I can bring souls across when I wish. Than is on semi-active duty and sometimes can be gone for days or weeks, depending on how he lets things lapse. We savor the time we have. Look, there are takeout menus in the drawer by the fridge. Call and order whatever you want. I'm going upstairs for a second. There's money in my purse by the door there. I wish I could give you a better answer, but I need to figure something out."

I raced into my office and saw the layout of the cards I had pulled for Azrael on my table. I took up the cards and shuffled them before I turned them over. The first thing I saw was the scarab. It was a solitary figure in the middle of the card, the beginning of something. I flipped over a second card and saw the ten of wands. The wands in this picture were mounted on the bases of statues of jackals that lined a pathway leading into a pyramid. I drew another one, the chariot. The one image that drew my attention the most was the sphinx at the front of the chariot. It had the form and face of a woman and a large cat. I pulled the last one. The tower. A bolt of lightning stuck and destroyed the top of a pyramid. I shook my head. I had drawn this card before. Apparently, it was still very relevant.

The path was laid out before me.

The clues were falling into place. The words of the figure in the cloak ran through my mind. *Look in the tombs.* Which ones? There were many. I pulled out the dagger Brenna gave me and examined it. A small golden ankh decorated the handle. I traced the symbol that meant eternity.

The answer had been in front of me all along.

CHAPTER EIGHT

The energy of the cards ran up my arm. My guides would have to wait. I was too much entranced with the cards regarding the path I walked. *I see it now. Why didn't I see it before? The shadow beasts are reanimated jackal mummies. If these mummies are coming back it only means one thing.*

A necromancer.

Sparrow was the only necromancer I knew. I pulled out my cellphone and dialed her number. *She can't be behind this. She mentioned she had a teacher.* After three rings her voicemail came on. I listened to her chipper voice and waited for the beep.

"Hey, Sparrow, it's Kerstin. I have a couple of things I need to discuss with you. Give me a call back when you get a second?" I hung up the phone and hoped that she was okay. I stared at the cards once more. If this thing was Egyptian in nature, then those were the tombs I'd have to look in. Maybe I had to go to Egypt and look in the actual tombs. I'd have to contact Azrael and find out if that was the truth.

"What am I doing to do?"

"What do you want to do?" The seductive voice said behind

me.

I didn't bother to look behind me, knowing that Mastema was in my room. "I'm going to find out what's going on. Did you think that I wasn't?"

"Of course not. It's in your nature to help people, and I mean that more than being a grim reaper of course."

This time I faced the direction where his voice was coming from. I shrieked. The front half of Mastema's head pressed between the dimensional crack. The corners of his mouth reached up halfway into his cheeks. His features were sculpted like any Roman bust would be to perfection. His golden skin and angled cheekbones were surrounded by a halo of golden hair with streaks of red and copper, changing color when he turned his head. His chocolate brown eyes were flecked with crimson and silver. I dared not look into them because they could capture and seduce anything. I was not about to be caught up in them.

"I take it I surprised you."

"How in world are you able to come through this way?"

"If I told you all my secrets, then what good would I be? Unless that's the boon you wish me to offer you? I can easily spill all of my secrets to you."

"I'm not going to ask you to tell me the secrets of the universe."

"But that wasn't what I offered. I said I would tell you all of *my* secrets and nothing more. I'm not sure you could handle them all anyway. I suppose you remember how to ask me questions. You were very good at it before."

He was right as always, but I wasn't going to tell him that. The last time I had asked him a question, I had been very specific. I had to be if I wanted to get the most truthful answer out of him. He *was* known to lie.

"I would *never* lie to you."

"What the hell are you doing here?" I ignored the fact he read my thoughts.

"I sensed your unease. I had the greatest urge to check on you."

"I'm not one of your demons you can control. You have no real feelings for me. You're just trying to seduce me. You shouldn't even be able to manifest here."

He sighed. It almost sounded like his heart was breaking. "Kerstin, that's where you're wrong. I can cross into this reality anytime I wish. It's a bit more strenuous to pull myself through because of the nexus you live upon. Than did well choosing this place. I have been trying to come through in all my finery, but the intersections of the universe make it disjointed. They change at all times, so finding a doorway to completely come to you is arduous."

"If you can come here anytime you wish, then what was that whole fiasco with the serial killer and collecting all those souls? You showing up just as disjointed body parts, doesn't work. That's just great. I'm sure you can scare my guests even more than they already are."

Mastema grinned. This time it almost seemed as though he meant it. "Remember what I said to you when you wounded me and shoved me back into the other realm? I don't need all the souls. You were only a means to an end. You started all of this."

"I didn't start the grim reapers going missing or mummified jackals hunting down the people I care about."

"True, you didn't set the hounds out. However, you're the one who set all of this in motion. Your death was the last key that had to be turned in the universal door. This is the culmination of events you set in motion. It's your destiny."

"My destiny isn't to bring about the death of grim reapers. Get the fuck out of here."

"Soon." He closed his eyes and flicked his serpentine tongue to taste the air. "I can taste your fear. It tastes likes cherries."

"My fear isn't relevant. You being here makes the situation worse. I don't need you terrorizing me at all hours of the day. I have things to do."

"You mean like discovering who is after the reapers in your graveyard? Or maybe trying to find your beloved angel? All of those answers are there for you if you ask me, and I'll grant you the boon you wished."

I threw up my hands. "I will never use the favor."

"That's what you say now, but wait and see. You'll need me more than you know."

"Just get out." I didn't need to listen to him anymore.

He laughed again and disappeared. None of his advice helped me. Although some of what he said made me question everything. *He said he could come into this world whenever he wanted. So why did he have the serial killer gather souls for him? What if Tobias was collecting spirits for someone else?* The dark figure in the cemetery had said that Nick's soul was in the well along with the essence of the other grim reapers. I thought about all those souls the serial killer collected by using the other mediums he had killed as catalysts. Where was this well? If it followed along with the rest of the theme it was in Egypt.

The doorbell rang downstairs. I went to get it and felt a cold breeze. In the doorway were both Moran and Raj. The skin sagged their faces, getting ready to drip off. "What's wrong with you? Is it the food you ate?"

"No," Raj answered.

"Then what is it? Is there something that I can do?"

Morana's dead eyes stirred something within me. There was something familiar about her I should have been able to see. "Nothing you can do. We just need to get to the other side. Can't you bring us now?"

"Sure, I can bring you, but aren't you afraid there are more monsters going to hurt you?"

"Yes, but we need to get back," Raj said.

"You're going to have to wait. I'm sorry. I have other things I have to worry about. Excuse me." They blocked my way. "I'm not playing right now. I need to get downstairs to the others and make sure they're okay."

A cold wall of power prevented me from passing. Their images wavered. Something other than the two ghosts was underneath the projection. I closed my eyes and pulled all of the power that was mine by right from being a grim reaper. I was not going to be bullied into thinking they could control me. My wings extended. Coldness expanded within me, and all the warmth flowed out of me. I was all death and nothing else.

"Get out of my way before I strike you down."

Morana laughed with the edge of insanity to it. "You're not going anywhere. You think you can show off because you have the power of death."

"That power was once mine as it was hers. Soon you'll be thrown aside just like all the others. Like we were once upon a time," Raj sneered.

"What do you mean that the power was once yours? You're not reapers," I snapped.

Raj's nose plopped to the ground. One of Morana's fingers rolled down a few steps. I wanted to see what was underneath their disguises. The first spirit who warned me said to look out for the ones who were disguised. Now I knew what she had meant.

They aren't spirits, but something entirely different and a whole lot more powerful.

How long had they been in the graveyard? Why hadn't Azrael and Than seen them? "How long have you been luring reapers to the jackals?" I asked.

"Wow, it took her long enough to put that together," Raj scoffed.

"Answer my questions. How many reapers have you lured?" The fury in my veins turned my blood to ice. The stairs creaked underneath me. A line of frost spreading out onto the wood and up the walls.

Morana stepped closer until she came up to my chest, but I sensed that she was taller than that. "More than enough to help free my master. More than enough to reach out into the cosmos and put a few little words into a few ears to tell them how to help free my master. It's such a shame Tobias never claimed your soul. It would have given him more power. But it wasn't your soul that he needed. It was your death."

"Tobias was working for you and not for Mastema." I took a step back. The cold drained away.

Raj nodded. "Oh, we just let him think that. Mastema's always supported our master. They go way back. Then things changed. It's time for him to take back what was stolen from him. You will set him free. He wants to meet you." He reached for me, but I willed myself out of the room and downstairs into the kitchen. Angela and Doni sat at the kitchen table.

"We have to go."

I grabbed Doni and pulled her from the chair. Angela took my outstretched hand. The two appeared in the doorway. Raj and Morana left bits and pieces of themselves along the floor. Angela and Doni tried to escape me, but I held onto them tight.

I couldn't take them to the graveyard. I had to get to Azrael. I couldn't take them into the center of the universe where there was nothing but a vacuum of space. *Brenna. Shit. She's in another reality. I don't know how it will affect Doni and Angela. I have to chance it.* I focused on her and prayed I would make it. When the world stop rushing by, the weight of the other reality descended. I landed inside of an office building. In it was all marble floors and gold leaf on the walls. It was old in architecture, but I could feel the ghosts that lingered in the walls of the place. Strong energy emanated from one of the suites.

"Where the hell are we? I thought we were safe at your house." Angela wiggled out of my grasp.

"It's a long story. Let me find my contact, and then I'll tell you all about it. I swear. Just don't tell anyone that I flew through time and space to bring you here."

"This doesn't feel like home," Doni whispered.

"That's because it's not." Energy hit me when I opened the door. It was so heavy it was almost tangible. A receptionist greeted me. Five or six other psychics filled the place. Each had their own table, decorated with crystals and tarot cards along with other little odds and ends that reflected the certain personality of the psychic.

"Can I help you?" the receptionist asked. Her fiery red hair stood out against her pale skin. A quick scan of her aura told me she was also a psychic.

"I'm looking for Brenna. Is she in?"

"I'm sorry. You just missed her. Did you have an appointment with her?"

The bell above the door rang. In walked an older black man who was lanky with a slight limp. He flashed me a smile as he went into the back to his table. Behind him Angela and Doni both came in. "No, I didn't have an appointment with her. We're friends, and I came in from out of town. I was hoping…"

"Excuse me." I jumped when I felt someone touch me. The man who had come in a minute ago stood next to me. His hair grayed at the temples and his dark brown eyes held a wisdom even beyond his years. This one was definitely an old soul.

"Yes," I said.

"Are you Kerstin?"

"I am."

"Good. Brenna told me to tell you that you should head over to her house. It's not far from here. I can show you if you like."

"But, Peter—" the receptionist's tone filled with panic. "You have an appointment in a few minutes and…"

"It's fine. They'll be okay to reschedule. It's one of my regulars, just tell Jerry to call back in an hour." He said to the receptionist. "Follow me, I'll show you the way." He opened the door so the three of us exited the shop, went to the elevator down the hall, and waited for it to open. When the doors yawned opened, the small space made me balk. I slipped in behind him. Doni and Angela also came in.

"Where are we going?" Angela asked.

"To see Brenna. She's…a friend of mine. She can help us with what's going on and keep you safe until all this blows over."

Peter studied me with those eyes, and a million questions bloomed in my mind. "How long have you known Brenna?"

"Not long. A year maybe. She helped me out of a tight situation. I was hoping she might be able to keep my friends safe from something else I've gotten myself involved in. How long have you known her?" We waited by the sidewalk to cross the street.

We were outside in the center of a bustling city. I wasn't sure exactly which one it was, but by the accents I heard around us I figured we were in the Northeast. I wanted to say it was Boston, but hopping from parallel worlds to different ones I wasn't going to make any assumptions. Cars honked their horns as people walked out in front of them. We followed the crowd and walked up the hill heading toward the large Capitol building with the golden dome on the top of it. Seeing that, I knew we were in Boston. This reality didn't feel as different as the one where Oliver had been in with Abner.

"I've known her for fifteen years now. Watched her grow up from college. We worked together for all those years. Then she went to New Orleans until she was called back here for other things. Now she owns the place. It's amazing to see how the darkness in a person can be overcome by the light and how much one has to fight their nature. The old place we were in was filled with all kinds of things, but the new space is much better." We came to the corner of the Boston Common. He guided us down the street while people seemed to stay out of our way. I kept waiting to see if Raj and Morana followed me. Peter knew something more about Brenna than what he let on.

"It's amazing how people can change. Or how the events of a decision made a long time ago ripples through time. But that doesn't mean you can't fix the outcome of that bad decision."

"This wrinkle keeps making things worse as I go along. It's never going to end."

He put a hand on my arm. "You'll see in the end it will all work out for you. Sometimes the worst things that you can ever imagine might have to happen before you completely wipe the slate clean. No matter how much you don't want it to. The world might seem crazy around you, but that doesn't mean you have gone crazy. Just remember that."

His advice meant something even if I didn't know the meaning. "I will. Thank you."

"Kerstin, where are we?" Doni asked.

"Boston, I think." I looked at Peter for confirmation.

"Yes. This is Boston. Did you not know that when you were planning on coming here?" Peter asked.

"It's a little complicated," I muttered as we walked past a row of Brownstones on the right side of the street and Boston Gardens on the left of us. The bushes were up around the top of the wrought iron fence and the trees ready to bloom. I hadn't been to Boston in a long time in my reality. I wondered if it was the same in this world.

"I've heard complicated before. From the looks of you, you've seen complicated a few times, too," Peter chuckled. "I doubt nothing can be as complex as Brenna's story."

"Ha! Don't be too sure. She might be…different and a good boss, but we've both had very singular events in our lives that have made us who we are. If you understand my meaning," I said to Peter.

"Well, I don't understand. Who is Brenna, and why are we here?" Angela stopped in the middle of the side walk. The day's events had worn on her. "I get you're psychic. We're supposed to be going somewhere safe, but how can Brenna protect us from those things?"

She didn't believe I could save her by bringing her here. I turned to her and held her shoulders. "Angela, I know things seem dire, but coming here is in your best interest. I don't want anything to happen to you. Brenna is like me in some ways. She can watch over you. She's more powerful than I am, and I hope she can point me in the right direction."

"She's another reaper?" she whispered.

"Yes, she is."

We went a few more blocks until Peter stopped.

"This is it. It was nice meeting you," Peter said.

"It was nice to meet you, too. How did you know?" I asked him.

He gave me a knowing smile. "It isn't hard to recognize a fellow colleague when you look hard enough."

Another reaper. He chuckled and walked until there was nothing left of him. Just like a grim reaper to make a stunning exit. I walked up the stairs and knocked on the door. It took a few minutes, but the door finally opened. I was expecting Brenna to open it. A gasp left my lips when I saw my boss standing there instead without a shirt on. I stared at his alabaster chest and his sculpted abs before I moved my eyes upward. His black hair reached halfway down his back. His dark eyes were tinted with a bit of red that faded away.

"Kerstin, what are you doing here?" The hard edge in his tone was not lost to me. The full effect of his cold power drained away when he realized I had company. "Who are these two lovely women with you?"

"Ahh…hi. I was looking for Brenna. I didn't realize that you'd be here. These are my friends. Can we come in?"

He moved aside and let us step in. I noticed then he was also barefoot. I had never seen him so casual. Once we stepped inside of the house, I realized this was his home as well as Brenna's. He would reside with her until she decided to also step into his world and take up her place by his side. She and I were more alike than I realized. We were both psychics, reapers, and angels of course. She even had her own encounter with the devil. Maybe she'd have some advice as to how I could get rid of him.

"Come in. Brenna's upstairs. I'll get her." Azrael went back upstairs.

"Staying here is supposed to keep us safe? How is that possible?" Doni asked.

"You know that man who just opened the door?" Angela gestured with her head in Azrael's direction.

"Yeah. What about him?" I said. "He's my boss, head honcho grim reaper, and an archangel. The woman who lives here is his female counterpart. She helped me a few months ago. This was the only place I could think of to bring you. The others don't seem to be able to crossover into this reality. If they do, well they haven't yet, so it gives us some time. It wasn't exactly what I planned, if that's what you were thinking."

I heard footsteps coming down the stairs as we waited in the living room. I glanced around and noticed the heavy curtains that ran the length of the windows that blocked out the light. A couch was behind us and a television on the other side across from us. I closed my eyes and felt I could relax a little. I felt my guides hovering near me and trying to get a message across. I wasn't in the mood for that either. I did get flashes of this house with another woman in it. This other woman lingered close to Brenna. The apparition glanced at me and flashed a warm smile before she faded away.

Her eyes lit up when she saw me. "Kerstin, I wasn't expecting you."

"Really? We went to the shop. Peter came in and brought us to the house."

"That's interesting. I didn't know he knew about you. I'll talk to him later."

"I hope he's not trouble. That wasn't my intention. He was very nice, and he cares about you very much."

Azrael glanced at us. "He knows what she is as she knows

what he is. The others know what we are, too. There is no reason to keep it a secret." He snapped his fingers, and he was clothed. It was difficult to remember he was an archangel. It was nice to think of him as a man. It also made me yearn to be with Than. My heart ached for him. I prayed he had gotten away from the jackals and avoided the other beast stalking me.

"Can I get you anything to drink? Or do we get right to it?" Brenna asked.

"I think we need to get right to it. I need some guidance. Azrael, told me to find out what's going on. I solved a couple of the mysteries. But other things I don't understand. Sir, I need to make sure that they," I gestured toward Angela and Doni, "are going to be safe. That's the reason I brought them here."

"Traveling between dimensions with passengers is against the rules. Telling them what you are is also against the rules. I should—"

"Azrael, cut Kerstin some slack. She's only doing what you would've done. If something was after me you would've gotten me out of there. Remember the time you brought me back to life after that werewolf got me. You had to give me your blood and anchor my soul so I wouldn't go off into the great beyond."

Azrael grunted, but the love glimmering in his eyes told another story. He slung his arm around her waist and kissed her swiftly before pulling away. "Saving you was the best thing I ever did even though at the time I didn't know why I was doing it. Fine. Kerstin, we can look after your friends. What do you know?"

I told him everything that had happened. Brenna listened intently. Doni and Angela recounted their encounters with the beasts as well.

"Do you think this large beast is the same one that attacked Oliver?" Azrael asked.

"I do. Abner gave me something. Hold on." I called upon my robe and pulled out the package the undertaker had given me. "I don't know what's in here, but it's something the reaper pulled off the thing that attacked her." I undid the bindings and peeled the brittle fabric away. Inside was a two-foot-long torn piece of leather. A few markings were etched into the material. I made out a symbol for a scale, and an ankh. Power tingled my fingertips. "Abner said it'd help me out. It obviously points me in the same direction that it was Egyptian and I need to look in the tombs. But does that mean actually going to Egypt? Do you recognize it?"

Azrael's pale complexion turned waxy. He clutched Brenna's hand. "It can't be. He was banished."

"What's the matter?" Brenna asked. "Azrael, talk to me."

The other angel shook.

"What the hell is going on?"

All of a sudden the house began to tremble. The lights flickered. The temperature plummeted ten degrees. Doni's teeth chatted. Azrael's eyes burned red. He hissed, showing his lengthening fangs. He growled and lunged at me, but Brenna grabbed ahold of him.

"Stop. Stop. You're going to hurt someone. You need to calm down. Now is not the time to lose control. Excuse me." She dragged and half pulled him into the other room. The others tried to look, but I followed them to see if I could help. Azrael said something incomprehensible. The look on his face was alien, demonic. Brenna tried to calm him, but she was losing her hold. She moved her hair from her throat and angled her neck. My boss struck the spot and fed from her. He truly was a vampire. I watched in awe as she uttered a small moan of pleasure. I realized that I was witnessing some sacred act between them. Azrael stared at me. I cringed and dropped my gaze only long enough to see him slip his hands through her hair and wrench her neck to the side and dig into it longer. Tears filled my eyes as I longed for Than and had a bad feeling about what was going on with him. I glanced back at the leather I had pulled from Abner's package.

"Forgive my manners." Azrael's cool demeanor had returned. He dragged his hand across his mouth, taking the remaining crimson from his lips. "I didn't mean to surprise you."

"That's fine. Can you tell me what this is? I haven't heard from Than. I'm worried about him. He should've been back by now."

If my boss had such a violent reaction to this old piece of leather, then it was something to be worried about. I touched the leather again and closed my eyes. My guides' influence won over, and I was hit with a variety of images. A hot, dry wasteland surrounded me. The strong aroma of jasmine assailed my senses. Then I couldn't breathe. I was plunged into the dark. I heard the rustle of chains and chanting. And tried to reach along the conduit that had been opened. Something strong and old hovered outside of my periphery. It tried to make contact with me. Something jostled me out of my trance.

I opened my eyes.

"Don't do that," Azrael instructed.

"Don't do what?" I asked.

"Whatever you were following, it could trace you back here. Neither of us wants that."

"Sorry. I didn't know."

"It's okay. Sit down, and I'll tell you what you brought. Ladies, forgive me if I scared you earlier. Brenna, can you get them something? I don't know exactly what you would like."

"Sure. Come into the kitchen with me." Doni and Angela

followed Brenna out of the room.

"Are you okay?" I asked him, lowering my voice a little because I figured this was something he didn't want to talk about because he hated getting too personal.

"I'll be fine. Sometimes I forget that strong human emotion can bring out the darker side of my nature. When you showed me that…collar, it brought back many other memories I thought had been hidden for a long time. They were not pleasant to say the least. It brought out—well you saw. Luckily, Brenna was here, and she quenched the thirst."

"I didn't mean to interrupt you and her. I wasn't trying to intrude on your time together."

My boss laughed. It was almost as devilish and seductive as the devil's. I wondered if all the archangels had that effect on others. It didn't hurt that he was handsome. Then again, I had complete strangers come up to me and tell me I was the most beautiful thing on earth. I attributed that to the angel part of me. I didn't see it except when I looked at Than because he was all angel to me and all I wanted.

"I realize I come off as aloof, but you can ask me advice. I was surprised you showed up here. That's all."

"But that doesn't mean you're going to answer my questions completely."

"True, but this time I'll tell you all that I know. Please sit." He gestured toward the couch. He took the bindings that the collar had been wrapped in and covered up the piece of leather. With a flick of his wrist the sickle that Tobias used last year to kill all his victims appeared. The blade sung in the air before he laid it down on the table beside the collar. "Do you have the small dagger Brenna gave you?"

"Sure." I fished it out of the pockets of my robe and laid it on the table. It was the same material as the sickle. Some dark metal that resembled onyx or jet, but it was metal and not stone. It was powerful enough to wound the devil and send him back to hell. I ran my finger over the blade. "I was thinking. It's something Mastema said to me."

"Did he appear to you again?"

"He did. He said that it doesn't matter where I am, he can come to me anytime. He finds it difficult to appear at the house because of all the different overlapping doorways and universes. Parts of him come through, so I can see or feel him."

"Has he come to you elsewhere, besides your house and Death's Dance?"

"No."

"Then that means he can only breach the realm in places where the veils are thin. I wouldn't worry about him. My brother is a master of manipulation. I should know as I nearly lost myself to him."

"You said something before about him being the father of demons, vampires, werewolves, and a whole bunch more things. Is that for all dark entities? How does that work across dimensions where there might be other kinds of vampires or creatures? They can't all be the same just as each parallel world and reality we visit isn't exactly the same, either."

He rubbed his chin, trying to figure out how much information he really wanted to reveal. "What did Mastema say to you?".

I loved how he just avoided my question. That wasn't anything new. Than did the same thing. Hell, I did the same thing when I spoke to souls. "At Death's Dance and when he was here last he said it. I didn't think anything of it back then. It pertains to what's been happening and what these other two spirits have said to warn me. I think he was telling me the truth. He said all of the souls he collected weren't for him. Mastema said that sometimes sacrifices had to be made for the bigger picture. Could he be working with someone else? The beast that came to me said I had only one more chance before I had to side with its master. Morana and Raj said their master wanted me. I'm in the middle of it again. What if on the grand scale of things this is all fated to happen?" I poured out my concerns to my boss. "Am I still paying for the bad decision I made as Lissandra? Is it a ripple effect? Mastema told me that all of it was tumblers in a lock, and my death was the last key that needed to be turned. What will the door unlock?"

Azrael sighed. "Sometimes actions trigger other events in the universe. I'm afraid that I had a hand in this, too. Before we get into all of that, let me start from the beginning."

"Okay."

He paced the living room. Laughter trickled from the kitchen. Brenna would watch over them until I could figure this all out. As Azrael walked by the table his image wavered between the man and the dark grim reaper. Each time the imposing figure came on him, I trembled as though he traipsed over my soul.

"The first being to hold the title of Death was the Archangel Gabriel. The position was created because human souls needed assistance in returning to the Universal Consciousness. We'll call it that because we all see it for something different. At first it wasn't much trouble for Gabriel to handle. Then humans evolved and started to believe in other things. You know that thought can shape reality. Energy is all around us, and it doesn't change."

"Of course."

"Mortals created their own mythologies giving rise to all different sorts of gods within certain mythologies. Some of the stronger thought forms, gods, became shape shifters moving from one religion to the next. Many of the death gods used to be reapers and became more gods than reapers. Ultimately, Gabriel couldn't keep up with the demand of all the souls. All the various deities gathered. It was decided they would handle all of their own affairs, so the death gods ruled over their own lands of the dead. Hades had his underworld. Marzanna had her lands. Erlik had his realm. Hel had her domain, but there was a ruler over them all.

"Anubis.

"He ruled over all of death, taking the position that I now hold. Things were fine. It ran smoothly for a long time. Then he began to go a little crazy, reaping souls and storing them in a large pit in his realm. He called it the Well of Souls. The Universal Consciousness, she decided it was time to do something about it and gathered the rest of the death gods. It was ruled that Gabriel would take the place once again until a suitable replacement was found. They sealed Anubis in his own dominion so that he couldn't escape. At that point, I had been lifted up and offered the position as Death. I was doing my job maybe for five or six hundred years and Anubis broke out. He tried to kill me with a sickle like this one. When that didn't work, he set his beasts upon me. That same collar was on one of the sphinxes that tried to injure me."

"That huge seven-foot monster is a sphinx? All the statue—"

"Humans always perceive things differently. That large animal stalking you is a sphinx. I killed all but one of them. The remaining one must be controlling the jackals. We fought once more. The other death gods were called along with a few angels who were loyal to me. They became reapers. If they didn't want this, they were allowed to continue on their realms helping souls in their realm through the barrier. The limbo, the cemetery as we know it. It just depends on the one who is taking the souls as to what it looks like."

"What happened to Anubis?"

"The well was drained of all the souls that remained. Anubis was put under the same rituals he passed onto humanity written in the Book of the Dead. Then he was placed in a sarcophagus and entombed. There he was supposed to stay forever. Parameters were set in place. Something so impossible that he could never get out."

I leaned back against the couch cushion. All of it sounded so unbelievable, but Azrael wouldn't lie about something like this. He told me the truth because he still flickered in and out of his grim reaper attire. "Apparently I triggered all these restrictions by accepting to take the souls from Death's Dance."

Azrael laid a hand on my shoulder. "Kerstin, this isn't your fault in any guise— past life or this one. I had a hand in all of this, too. I allowed you to become a reaper again. I told you to clean up your mess regarding Death's Dance. At the time it felt like the right thing to do. I made you human once more and reinstated you as the reaper you are. You might've been the key, but I turned the locks. Don't blame yourself. I need you sharp. There's a reason why only *you* can see those death gods and why Mastema is coming to you. You're different. You straddle the boundaries of the living and the dead. It makes you resonate on a different frequency. I hadn't really noticed before now. It has to be because of everything that you've been through. Now we know what's going on. I know you're worried about Than. You love him the way I love Brenna. If anything happened to her, I would be lost. When I took over for Anubis, there were others in heaven and in hell who resented the fact I was given the position because of what I am. Vampires are another form of demon to many angels. They asked the One, 'how you could lift up something so evil into a position of such grandeur? Wouldn't he taint the office?' Her answer was that there was darkness in everything, but within me there was light too. I was the best one for the job. Sometimes we don't write our fate. It's woven into a tapestry that even the great one can't change. I just wish that it didn't have to happen to you."

This all started from one stupid choice made centuries ago. "So even though you're a vampire you proved all of the other angels wrong."

"Almost. There was one. He fell and became one of Mastema's minions the way that I did. I nearly succumbed to the evil in me. Brenna saved me. I even stole the part of her that was different from the other vampires, like me, and set it into the heavens to create a star. Her love saved me. Even in all my anger, love won out.

"You know most of the angels don't have souls, so they don't really feel. Spend enough time among the cosmos, even with a soul, and you'll forget as well. All those human emotions fade into the back of your mind. Being with Brenna makes me remember, and I get to be all that I am."

"Will she ever join you as a reaper?"

He glanced into the kitchen. "One day. But her destiny is here, helping people. The same way you guide people through life. You're very similar. I think that's why I was drawn to you this last time. I saw in you what I see in her. And that's why I gave you the chance to be with Than and to live once more. Once I made the choice, I knew it was the path of your destiny."

"That's great and all, but what happens now? Do I end up dying? Do you?"

"I don't know, but remember that reading you did right

before I showed up in your bedroom? You said death was coming. Well, you were right. Anubis is death. Does that mean you or I will die? Both of us or just him? I don't know. It means we'll have to face him."

"What about Than?" I couldn't see my existence without him.

"We're going to find out together what happened to him. Brenna will watch out for the women you brought here. Although, you really shouldn't have brought them across dimensions. It could've been dangerous."

"I know, but I didn't want them to die because of me like those poor EMTs, or look at what happened to Nick. He's a shell, and according to that spirit his soul is in that well. I can't let him suffer any longer."

"You realize those warning you were really death deities against Anubis. Just as the ones who were luring in the other reapers are the ones in league with him."

It did make sense. "When I asked Morana and Raj how long they'd been doing this, they said it'd been awhile. I bet they've been culling reapers for a long time. Being angels that might have given Anubis enough power to start him trying to get free."

"When you were in the graveyard, did you see anything odd?"

"Besides the jackals trying to kill me? A cloaked woman stood in front of a desert. It was flat, brown and yellow in the distance. I didn't see any tombs, but I didn't get very far because the howls started."

"Then that's where we go."

CHAPTER NINE

"**N**ow?"

"Why not? The more time we give him, the stronger he becomes. We can't risk him escaping. It could mean the end of everything. He believed the whole world should be dead and humans should learn to live in his kingdom. Anubis wanted to mummify all of them, cast aside the other gods, and proclaim himself ruler. He's unpredictable."

"And we're going to go up against him alone?" I asked. "He—" Pain engulfed me. I collapsed and screamed until my throat was raw. My nerves were being frayed, and my guts twisted. I clawed at my skin to make it stop. Azrael clasped my arms and held me. The pain ceased. My entire body shook, and tears streamed down my cheeks. It took me a minute to find my voice.

"What's going on? Tell me," Azrael said.

Brenna ran in from the kitchen followed by my friends. They stood back. Azrael held up his hand to keep Brenna away. I bathed in his cool power before I could talk. "Pain. I was freezing and burning at the same time. I don't know where it came from."

"It's okay. You're safe."

Something crawled underneath my skin. It started off as an itching, and moved up my arm. I pushed up my sleeve. A lump the size of a silver dollar undulated under my flesh. Each time it moved it bubbled up the skin until it was transparent enough the green and black shimmer of the thing could be seen. It moved again showing the thing beneath my flesh. It had six legs and was oval shaped with pinchers. Another itch started in my leg. Another came from my stomach. I went to scream, but one of them crawled up my esophagus I choked. I broke away from Azrael. The agony returned. The insect settled on the back of my tongue until I spit it out.

"Brenna, stop it before it gets away." Azrael gestured to the scarab skittering across the floor.

The skin stretched along the left side of my face. Another one moved under my cheek, around my eye socket. Its feet and its antenna tickled my eyeball until it was a dark spot in my vision and it scuttled out.

"Kerstin, you have to break your connection to Than. What do you have on you that's part of him?" He stomped on one of the scarabs. I tried to speak, but another one started to eat its way out of my neck. I tried to pull the necklace out. Azrael grabbed it. A gush of blood spilled down my front. Air rushed over the inside of my throat. Another bloody scarab scurried across the floor. Azrael yanked the necklace off and lobbed a ball of purple energy at it. Once the pulse hit the feather Than had given me, the pain and the scarabs stopped.

The damage done to my body was great. I couldn't see out of my left eye. I couldn't speak. Three inch holes dotted my arms and legs where the bugs had eaten their way out. Azrael laid his hand on my head. His energy moved through me and healed me as he had done with Oliver. When he withdrew his energy from me, I could no longer feel Than.

"Oh, God. He's dead. They killed him," I sobbed. The emptiness consumed me. What was I without him? He was my other half.

"We don't know that," Azrael said. "I'm sorry, Kerstin. Anubis was trying to get my attention. I think you made contact with him earlier when you touched the collar and were barraged with images."

"Wonderful."

"He's using Than against you to get to me because he knows you're a reaper. I'm so sorry you had to endure this. Stay strong for me. I need your help to go up against him. Can you do that?"

My resolve hardened. There wasn't anyone else to go up against Anubis. I couldn't risk any other grim reaper. Oliver had gotten hurt because of it. The sphinx followed me and found him. It was tough to believe that creature was the one the Egyptians had carved and guarding the Pyramid of Khufu. At least it wasn't making me solve a riddle so I could pass. *If Than is dead, he'd want me to fight for him. He'd want me to keep on going. He did for me when he watched me reincarnate all those years. He has a soul. It means I can find him again.*

"Do you remember before when I asked you to release me from my duty?"

My boss nodded. "When you were Lissandra, yes I remember. Why do you bring it up?"

"I was just thinking. You let me go so I could move beyond the veil. I remember going a little crazy as I passed through the fog to the other side. You said the well of souls was like the passage between this world and the other. Moving between the worlds changed me, didn't it? What about the well? You said it's a portal, too."

"It used to be. But it was cut off a long time ago when the souls were drained."

"What if we can get Anubis into the well? Seal him in there and close whatever door he's opened."

"It's not a bad idea, but it's dangerous. It could make him crazy. Even a few seconds in it could alter someone in ways we don't know. It's more than your aura or your soul vibrating on a different frequency. It's not something you want to tamper with. The concentration of energy within it is more than any one grim reaper can handle. Even me. It took a collective of angels and death deities to close it down before. I can only imagine what he did to be able to open it back up. It must've taken a great sacrifice to restart the well, open the portals, and break him out of the sarcophagus."

"If Tobias was really helping him and not Mastema, then there could be others on the outside helping him we don't know about." The image of who it might be flashed in my mind. "Sparrow."

"Who is she?" Azrael asked.

"Wasn't she one of those other psychics at the convention we were all at?" Doni asked.

"Yeah. I remember her. My mother and I stopped at her table because it was covered with skulls and other dark stuff. I wanted to get my palm read, but my mother dragged me away," Angela chimed in.

I caught a bit of movement out of the corner of my eye. Another scarab scampered toward Doni and Angela. I lobbed a small energy ball at it. It singed the floor and the bug screamed. The scarabs couldn't get out. I remembered what Abner had said about the scarab that had been in his curio cabinet among the other things. It could eat someone from the inside out. *What did it do to Than?* Tears burned my eyes. My grief turned to rage. I wanted to rip apart time and space to undo what had been done. The floor shook beneath me as I pulled in the energy of the cosmos. My fingers curled into fists. Azrael grabbed my wrist.

"Kerstin, don't lose control now. I know you want to take out your anger for what happened to Than. We still have foes to face. Why don't you spend the night here to recover? I'm sure your friends need a minute to recuperate. Besides, there are some things I need to gather. Can you do that?" Azrael asked.

I drew back in the power. The current of electricity ran underneath my skin waiting to be released. He was right. I was exhausted, and I needed time to process the emptiness lingering in my heart. "Okay."

He walked over to Brenna and said something to her before he disappeared. "I'm going to show you two to the guest rooms upstairs. Follow me." She left the room, and I walked over to the coffee table. I picked up the dagger Brenna had given me, wound my hair up, and slipped it through the bun so I wouldn't lose it. I folded up the collar and thought about burning it. If it had once bound a sphinx then there had to be some power still left in it. I trailed my fingers over the sickle and picked up the handle. I remembered the feel of its cold energy and could almost hear the screams of those souls that had fallen underneath its blade. The energy of it was tainted with the evil and the deaths that Tobias had used it for. All those souls were still stuck in that well if they hadn't already been used up. I needed to use this on Anubis. If it had once belonged to him, then it would take his head. *He'll know we're coming. There has to be a way to get into his realm without being detected. The collar's a direct link to him. Death is death. At the very core, we're connected somehow.*

Brenna came back downstairs and leaned against the

doorway. "This wasn't how I expected to spend my afternoon off."

"Sorry. I didn't mean to bring this to your doorstep. I didn't know where else to go."

"It's all right. You did the right thing. Don't listen to Azrael regarding crossing the dimensions. I'm sorry about Than. I haven't met him, but I can tell you love him very much. I know how it feels. I almost lost Az a few times."

"You lost someone else too that you care about."

Brenna's cheeks reddened too. She ran her fingers through her dark brown hair. "I didn't realize you'd seen her."

"What's her name?"

"Veronica, she was…I became a vampire because of her. It's a long story. She died, and it nearly killed me. I turned my back on everyone I loved. Don't do that. It took Azrael walking away from me to realize what I'd lost. Peter helped pull me through."

"He was the one who brought us here."

"He's still looking out for me no matter what. He passed away last year. It was rather sudden. I never saw it coming. Azrael offered him the position without me knowing about it. When Peter appeared as a reaper I nearly lost it, but I'm glad that he's here. He was my mentor when I first started at the Tearoom. You would've liked him. We're very much alike, you and me."

"That's what Azrael said."

"Come on. Let's go outside and get some air. You can use it."

Being stuffed in a human body was more confining than it had been before. I walked outside into the night with Brenna. I felt more of a kinship with her than I did to the other reapers, even Than. We went to the side of the house and went up another staircase that led up to the roof. When I looked at the stars, they were the same as they were in my reality.

"Your world seems very similar to mine. The stars are in the same place."

She glanced up and smiled. "It's disconcerting to see different constellations when you move to another world or another universe. But half the time you don't stop to think about it because one half of you might be split and collecting souls and the other half is off doing something else."

"I haven't really gotten to the part of splitting myself into different pieces yet. I have a hard-enough time reconciling everything that's happened to me in past lives and being smooshed together."

"I know the feeling. Sometimes going into a dozen pieces makes you a little thin."

"It surely does. I remember doing it from before when I was Lissandra." An airplane passed overhead. The sounds of the city were a little muted from the roof. A bench and a small waterfall sat in the corner. Potted plants and trees were scattered around with a table and a couple of chairs. There was an arbor with night blooming flowers that hung down it. The scent was pregnant in the air, sweet and sticky, something I would think to smell from the south. "Peter said you were in New Orleans for a little while."

"I was. It was a second home to me."

"That's right. I remember you told me if I ever went down there to look up Marie Laveau. I guess New Orleans isn't as different here as it is in my reality."

"New Orleans is New Orleans just like the Bermuda Triangle is what it is. No matter what universe you go into it's always going to be what it is. It's an intersection of worlds, times, realities—you name it. Why do you think so many crazy things happen there?"

"Pfft. You should come to my house."

"Azrael mentioned it was a nexus."

"Yeah, enough so that parts of Mastema randomly show up

when he wishes to be frisky."

"Don't let him get to you. He's an ass."

"I know," I chuckled. "How do you and the boss get along with him split into infinity times two running around the universe delivering souls? Sorry. That's kinda personal."

"No. It's okay. It's nice to have someone to talk to who understands what it's like to be a grim reaper. You're a psychic, too, so that makes it even better. You understand the pull between the higher realms and the darker ones because we walk the line between life and death. It's grueling at times. I don't take many souls over to the graveyard, just a few here and there. I wanted to live my life, and being a vampire, I have forever. Being an angel, too…well I try not to think about it much."

"Can you walk in the daylight? Most vampires can't, or at least that's the myth."

"I can. Only because I'm different than the others of my kind. Most have two personalities, the vampire and the human. The vampire wants to placate the master that turned them. In most cases the vampire personality dominates and wipes out the human. Or they struggle, and it drives them insane. Sometimes they come to a harmonic union. That was the way with Azrael's only child he ever turned. That's another story. Veronica battled with her vampiric side all the days of her life, but she's free of that."

"She watches out for you, though."

"She comes and goes as she wishes. It was hard at first when she left, but she's always in my thoughts."

"Of course I am." A woman stood next to me with long brown hair and pale skin with the faint luminesce of the otherworld behind her.

A faint blush colored Brenna's cheeks. "Veronica, what are

you doing here?"

She trailed her fingers down Brenna's cheek. "I had a feeling I was needed."

"There's nothing you have to do."

"Really? You need someone who can move among the dead and not be noticed. That's something that I can do."

"What are you proposing?" I asked.

"Veronica, you don't need to endanger yourself. You need to be resting or whatever you do on the other side," Brenna said to her.

Veronica took on a more solid form. She drew Brenna into a hug and kept her close. Tears glistened in Brenna's eyes. Veronica brushed her lips along the other woman's before turning to me. "Kerstin, I heard what you were saying. I have an idea on how to get you into the other realm."

"No. I can't let you martyr yourself. They could—"

Veronica held up her hand. "There's no trying to talk me out of it. This could be your one shot. Don't do anything until you hear from me."

Brenna tried to protest again, but Veronica faded away.

"I'm sorry. I swear I never said anything to her."

"It's fine. Veronica was always stubborn. She'd never listen to me, but then again she always said that I was the obstinate one. I trust her. I don't know if I could lose her twice. She never had to deal with some of the things that I've had to deal with. But she's free of all that, and I'm proud that she is. We need to watch over your friends and keep them safe."

"Thanks."

"For what?"

I shrugged. "For being there. Like you said. You understand what's going on. And for taking us in."

"What are friends for?"

What were they for indeed? I didn't have many, and I had to protect them. I pulled my cell from my pocket, hoping to see a message from Sparrow. The screen showed me the time and the e-mails I had. Oddly enough, I got decent reception in a different reality. I'd have to tell my phone company next time I upgraded.

"I'm going to go check on your friends. I don't have much for dinner, but I can order out."

She started to leave, but I caught her arm. "Brenna, you died. I mean when you became a vampire. It changed you in some way. It messed with the vibration of your soul and the way that you affect things. Didn't it?"

"Of course it did. All death does."

"You drink blood. You must've killed people in your time. If you could go back, would you?"

She sighed and stared at the stars the way I had before. "Kerstin, you don't have to tell me about wanting to turn back time. I've had those same thoughts. We can't go back and mess with time. And yes, I've died several times. It seems to be a prerequisite to be a reaper or at least one who has a soul. You might find it ominous at what you have to do. There are a lot of things that I'd try to reverse. In order to do that, I'd change all of the events up to this point. The last ten years have been wonderful. Azrael's learned what it's like to be a man and forget about being the angel. It's been good for him, and for me. I feel human with him. I think you feel that way with Than."

If I changed anything in the past, then I might not be with Than. Fury boiled underneath my skin the way those scarabs burrowed under my flesh. *Anubis won't get away with murdering the man I love.* When I searched our connection emptiness came back to me. I was hollow inside except for the rage. I recalled the first time I saw him in my dreams as a child, a robed figure that stood by a tree or within the graveyard. I never feared him. He was just a lone figure who watched over me. Than was the one thing I always counted on. It didn't matter if I was having a bad day, then he would be there when I dreamed. He risked his life to save me from Sariel. It was time I repaid the favor. It'd be so easy to jump into the abyss widening in my mind and lose myself to the madness that loomed on the edge of my consciousness. I couldn't go fall into the deep hole yet. Than had to be avenged.

"Yes. That's what love is. There are more things I need to do yet before I end up losing it completely."

"You won't go off the deep end. We'll catch you before you fall." Brenna squeezed my shoulder before leaving me alone on the roof to my own thoughts. The sounds of the city kept me anchored for now.

My revenge would come.

CHAPTER TEN

We stayed at Brenna's for a day before Azrael returned. Brenna told him about Veronica and how she had gone off on her own. Angela and Doni were entertained, but I could tell they were waiting for the other ball to drop. Truthfully, I waited for the other death deities to appear too, but they never did. I pursued a few books on mythologies boasting death gods and tried to figure out who were the ones at my house. The words blurred together, and all I thought about was Than. Brenna tried to keep me distracted with chit chat, and even asked me if I wanted to do a few readings at her tearoom. However, I wasn't about to read people when it was a struggle to breathe. Agony and fury made up my soul. I ran over the events. I thought what Than had endured. How had it been for him? What had Anubis done to him? How had he withstood all of it?

"Kerstin, was this one of them?" Angela asked. She pushed the book over to me. Gods and goddesses were listed alphabetically. I scanned the page, but the letters jumbled together. One name jumped out at me. Azrael had said it before. Marzanna in Polish or Morena in Czech, Slovak, or Russian. *That sounds very similar to Morana. She's associated with winter and rebirth, a goddess of death.* I couldn't find anything describing what she looked like, but my gut told me it was her.

"This was the one that came to me as a little girl." I tapped the page. "She claimed her family was murdered. She's very convincing. I invited her into the house. When she was at the cemetery on the property the other ghosts never wanted to be around her. It never dawned on me. There was so much going on. I assumed that it was something to do with Mastema and how he keeps popping up inside my head."

"You said that there was another one that looked like a baseball player. His name was Raj?" Doni asked.

"Yeah. He had a donkey or buffalo on his hat. The uniform was blue and gold. He was Indian with a New York accent. His skull was bashed in with a bat. Two reapers were taking him across. He must've led them somewhere so the jackals could either take them or the others would."

Doni flipped a few more pages in her book while I moved backward through mine. I came to a drawing of a woman standing in an underground cavern with jets of fire in the background. People walked past a stone throne. I knew this place. The caption read Hel standing dominion over Hell. She brought me to her realm from that run-down house in the woods. She was a Nordic death deity.

"Ahhha!" Doni exclaimed.

"What did you find?" Angela slammed her book shut.

Doni showed me the picture of a man riding a buffalo. He had dark hair, a golden hat, and blue skin. There was no real resemblance from the picture to the young man who had eaten everything in my fridge.

"It says here that his name is Yama or Yamaraja. He's a

Hindu god of death. Do you think it could be him?" Doni asked.

"I think so. That just leaves one more, and she is the one who helped me, but I don't know her name or what she looked like," I explained.

"Didn't you say that you were given advice from another spirit?" Doni asked.

"Yeah, but I figured out who that is. She's Hel." I gave the book to Doni and Angela so they could see the drawing I zeroed in on.

A blast of cold air filled the room. Azrael held Veronica in his arms. Her dress was shredded. Red welts and scratches marred her appearance.

"Oh God, Veronica." Brenna hurried over to her as Azrael set Veronica down on the couch.

"She's going to be okay, Brenna. You have to give me room to heal her."

I squeezed her shoulder. Azrael sat next to Veronica with a hand on her forehead. Within a few seconds her glow returned and the scratches were healed.

"Where did you find her? How did you find her?" Brenna asked.

Veronica moaned. Her eyes fluttered opened. "Thank you. I thought I was a goner there for a few."

"What happened?" I asked.

Azrael moved out of the way. Brenna rushed to be at her former lover's side. They embraced and said a few things to one another that I couldn't hear, but it didn't seem to bother Azrael one bit. Brenna kissed her lightly before pulling away, and Veronica was brighter than ever.

"I went into the graveyard and walked around until I saw a reaper. I hid as the sphinx came after it. The reaper tried to get away. The creature clawed his chest. Then it took the reaper into its jaws and walked further into the cemetery. I followed. It passed into the wasteland. I tried to follow. A figure appeared all in black and told me I couldn't pass. I asked why. She said it wasn't my place because it was only for the lost. I asked her if she'd warned you about looking in the tombs. She didn't say anything at first. Baying erupted from the desert. These black shapes rushed toward me. I begged her to help. She said to meet her in hell. One of the jackals jumped me. I ran as fast as I could back toward the veil. They pursued me. I guess that was when I collapsed. Their claws burned where they had gotten me. I called out for Azrael. It was fortune you found me. Thank you for healing me."

"Do you know what she means by meeting her in Hell?" Brenna asked.

"I do. Kerstin, we should go," Azrael answered.

I nodded. It was time to make sure Than was avenged and Anubis paid for what he did. I'd put him back in his sarcophagus, or I was going to kill him outright. We had weapons to kill death. This time he would face the end of his existence no matter what it took.

Azrael kissed Brenna. "Keep them safe. Veronica, rest here for a little while."

She nodded. I knew the true meaning behind his request. Stay here for me in case I don't come back, because Brenna is going to need someone. "Of course."

"Ready?" Azrael asked.

I summoned my reaper garb. The full power of my office descended over me. I also felt more powerful than I had before. Azrael stood next to me also in skeletal attire. "Um... boss did you do anything here? Am I a full reaper again?"

"Let's just say you got a promotion for all the hard work

you've been doing. I can only give you so much until you come back on full time. You're going to need everything you have and then some. You're still as you are, a hybrid, half human and half reaper, but now you're a lieutenant."

Wow, I had moved up in the death world. "Let's go."

Azrael spread his wings. I followed him. Reality moved by so quickly I barely paid attention to my surroundings until we landed in the barren place that I had been before with Hel. They had called it Hell, and I could see why. They didn't know true Hell because Mastema wasn't in it. We stood on a long ledge. Below us loomed endless darkness. The throne was crumbling. The cauldron was dented and half gone. Beyond that was a blank brown wall. The light that illuminated the cavern came from the columns. The carvings on them were faded. If this was truly Hel's domain, then she had lost her power. What did the other gods do when they lost their power?

A figure paced back and forth in a long robe. The hood of her cloak covered her face and hung down her body as though she was in mourning. She went to her knees before Azrael.

"Lord Azrael. It is an honor. I didn't realize…"

"It's all right, Nephthys. Please get up. You've never had to kneel before me. None of you have. In your own right you've always been death and attached to this office."

The woman rose. I didn't realize he knew her right off. Her gaze traveled to me. "You were following the sphinx."

"Yes, I'm Kerstin. I didn't realize at the time you were a goddess." I pushed the hood off, revealing my true face.

"Can you tell us what's going on?" Azrael asked her. "I thought he was entombed. You were supposed to be watching over him."

"I'm sorry," she whispered. "I've guarded the entrance as

you bade me. I didn't know what was going on until it was too late. Those loyal to him found another way in and fed him souls. They started restocking the well and taking grim reapers. I tried to confront him once, but he…he…" she broke down in sobs.

Azrael put his arm around her. He kept her close while she wept and drew back her hood. The echo of her beauty remained. Now she was weathered skin and sunken eyes that were nothing more than blue raisins. Her hair was woven up in an elaborate crown. Her gums had pulled back from her teeth. Part of her face was normal. Her hair was jet back. Her fingers were long and thin with nails that scratched along Azrael's skin. She had been mummified.

"That bastard," he muttered.

"I'm not the beauty you once remember." Nephthys pulled her robe closer to her body.

"You're always going to be beautiful to me." He pressed his lips to hers in a brief kiss. "Once this is over, I'll restore you. He never should've done this to his own mother."

"He's not the son I bore."

"Anubis is your son?" I asked. "Sorry, I don't know much about Egyptian deities or mythology."

"It's okay, Kerstin. The world's changed. I tried to make him stop what he was doing, but he captured me. The Well of Souls is almost full. The Fallen one came to him some time ago. They struck up a deal. The Fallen one gave Anubis power to resurrect the sphinx to its full grandeur. They talked about keys in a lock. I didn't hear all of it. It was only then that—" she gestured toward her face.

The tendons on the side of Azrael's neck bugled. He curled his fist into a ball. The temperature plummeted until my breath came out as vapor. Mastema helped plan all of this. His words to me made more sense now. "Why would Mastema help Anubis retake the station of death?"

"Because he's a jackass that likes to stir up trouble."

"But why?" I asked Azrael.

"There doesn't have to be a reason with him, Kerstin. He likes to put things on end and stir them up. There's no rhyme or reason to it. Why does he haunt you?"

"Because he wants me to use the boon he gave me," I replied.

"If you ever did, what do you think will happen?" Azrael gripped his scythe.

"That I'm screwed. I'm tied to him forever because he did a favor for me. I never promised anything to him in return except that kiss so I could figure out what was going on with the serial kill. Not that it did much good."

"You did what you had to do in the moment. It might not have been the best choice, but you needed information. If he did a binding contract with you where he isn't supposed to get anything in return then he won't take it. He's truthful when it comes to that, but Mastema's a mischievous son of a bitch. If he can find a way to turn the universe on its head, then he will. He's the epitome of evil. Nothing can stop him. As long as darkness and evil are in the world, then he will exist. You can wound him, but you can never truly kill him. Trap him yes, but nothing else."

I nodded, understanding the issue of balance in the universe and how it had to be kept. Mastema swore I would need to use his favor, and then he would own me. There was nothing that I wanted from him at all except the revenge that Than deserved. If he was involved in Than's demise, then devil or not, he'd regret appearing to me in the first place.

"What do we do?" I looked at them both.

"How full is the well?" Azrael asked.

"Brimming. He has enough power. He's been waiting for the right time. He's been waiting for you. I'm sorry, Azrael. I didn't have a choice."

The wall before us exploded in a shower of rubble. I screamed at the sudden noise and tried to will myself away. The great weight of the rocks pinned me under them. I tried to move them off me. All senses were cut off, and then there was only darkness.

It took me a moment to realize I was awake. The weight of the stones pressed upon me, but I heard them shifting. A muffled voice yelled to me.

"Don't worry. I'll get you out."

A small hole of light shone through the darkness of my stone prison. I looked up and saw Nephthys. And then I saw another familiar face. Oliver.

"Hey, Kerstin. Fancy seeing you here."

"What are you doing here?" I asked.

"I heard Azrael's call for backup. Took me a bit to find you. Wow, I haven't been to Hel in a long time. This place certainly has gone downhill. I appeared right as the portal was blown wide open. They captured Azrael and pulled him back through the gateway. Damn, I thought all those gods were locked up in purgatory. Then Nephthys told me Azrael was knocked unconscious, and here I am. I never thought anything could get to the boss."

Nephthys removed a large rock and offered me her hand. I took it as she pulled me to freedom. Fresh air blew over me, and I cleared my lungs from all the dust. I glanced at the fallen goddess and tears brimmed in her eyes as she looked at me.

"I didn't have a choice. Anubis has my heart. One quick stab, and then I'm done for. I don't want my existence to end. I'm sorry."

I tried to be sympathetic for her, but I couldn't feel it. I glanced at Oliver. "Are you coming with me?"

He scratched his head. "I don't know. This really isn't my thing. Going up against gods and such. I'm sorry, but I have my undertaker to look after and his assistant. There are some things brewing there. I can't be quite sure. I've heard of other undertakers being killed."

"I understand. Thank you for helping free me."

Oliver flashed me a half smile. "Hope to see you around." He winked out.

The bones popped in my shoulders when I rolled them. It was time to face Anubis and make him pay. "I need to get into his lair. I don't care if he's your son. I don't care he has your heart. If you want to redeem yourself, it'd be a good start in getting me into Anubis's tomb. You told me to search the tombs, so I know that's where I have to go. Or was that something that you told me to throw me off the scent. Tell me the truth." I summoned my scythe and felt the hard handle in my palm.

"I—" she panicked and her raisin eyes widened. I pressed the scythe to her neck.

"One stroke and this could take your head and end your existence."

"Your scythe can't do anything to me."

I vanished the weapon and summoned the sickle to her throat. "How about this?"

"Where did you get that?" The fear in her voice was evident.

"What do you say? Are you going to help me or not?" I pushed the blade into her skin until she gagged. "I'm sorry. I'm frustrated. I understand you want to protect your son. Nonetheless, you know he's going to try and take over the world or whatever his diabolical plans are. We must stop him. I *have* to stop him."

Nephthys wiped her eyes with withered fingers. I slipped the sickle back into my robes and ran my hand down my chest, hoping for the comfort of Than's feather. But it wasn't here nor was Than. I tried not to think about him, but the hole remained and nothing would ever fill it.

"You lost someone."

"Yes. Your son killed him. He's the reason I'm here. Right now, I need to rescue Azrael. If you feel any loyalty to him, then you owe him this."

She grimaced. "I can take you to a side entrance where you can slip into his tomb. I won't be responsible for what happens there."

"Fine."

"This way." Nephthys led me to a small shelf that wrapped around the wall. I pressed my hand against the stone, feeling my way along and trying not to fall. If I did, I wasn't sure where I would end up going down. At least I had the wings to lift me back up.

We walked for several hours. Each time we moved into a new area the pressure change pressed down on me until finally we came to a dead end.

"Through there. It'll lead you into the lower level of his pyramid. Go up four levels and you'll find his dungeons. I can't help you anymore. I'm sorry." She stepped off the ledge, and the darkness swallowed her.

I faced the wall of black stone. An electric current ran up my arm when I touched it.

CHAPTER ELEVEN

I took a deep breath and moved through the wall. I could barely see on the other side. Screams of souls wrenched my heart. I would free them no matter what the cost. I threw a small energy ball into the air, giving me enough light to see by in the dungeon. Rows of locked cells stretched before me on both sides. I peered inside of one. A skeletal figure lay curled up on the floor in the corner.

"Hello?"

The creature looked up. As it moved each bone cracked. Two long fangs jutted over its lips. This was not a regular soul. "Help," it whispered. It crawled over the stone floor and reached up its hand to me.

I tried to slip my way through the door, but it was impervious to any of my powers. "I can't."

"Kill me," it pleaded. "Bring me peace."

"I'm sorry. I can't. I'll come back for you. I promise." I backed away from the door and looked into a couple more cells. Each was the same. They were filled with the same type of shriveled beings so I couldn't tell what they had been before. Anubis had been using them, draining them of their power or vitality. Footsteps echoed in the stone fortress. I extinguished the light and slid into the shadows. A large guard walked through the hallway carrying a spear. A scream erupted from somewhere in the tomb and shook my bones. It was the sound of someone being tormented, and that someone was Azrael. If he died, then what would become of us reapers? A multitude of questions plagued my thoughts. His shriek gave me something to follow, so I wouldn't be lost in this endless maze.

I walked through the passageways until I came to the room where Azrael was being held. Light blue flames flickered in sconces along the dark walls. The mural behind him was filled with paintings of jackals and pictures of the other death gods. I slid into the darkness and saw the two gods who had been to my house. They stood before him in the same melting guises and giggled. Morana sliced at Azrael's chest with a knife. Small crimson trails painted his flesh. He screamed as the blade ran across his skin.

"You really think you can claim rulership over all of us gods? Did you think you could exile us all those years ago? You have no idea what's coming to you."

"Let me go now, and I'll make sure your existence isn't ended when I get out of here." Azrael struggled to free himself of his bonds.

Raj dug into his stomach with a hooked blade. His wounds slowly healed, and they would start once more. Morana's girlish giggles set me on edge. Nothing like this was ever going to happen again. I slipped out from my hiding spot and struck down Morana, catching her across the back. She gave out a strangled scream and dropped the knife. Raj turned around and slashed at me. I jumped out of the way of his weapon before it touched my cloak.

"You'll never make it out of here alive. He's going to cremate you," he yelled.

"I don't think so. And you won't be going anywhere either." He lunged at me, but I swung the scythe. It took his head in one slice. His body flopped to the floor and hit as ashes. I vanished the weapon and went over to Azrael. His manacles were made from the metal as the weapons I carried. I tried to undo them, but they weren't budging.

"Don't worry about me, Kerstin. Find Anubis. Be careful of the sphinx. He's still around here," Azrael warned.

"I can't just leave you here."

"I'll be fine. I have a few tricks up my sleeve that even you don't know about."

"Okay. Where should I go?"

"There's a passage just over there. I don't know how many are there, so be careful."

"I was in the dungeons. He's been draining power from creatures, I don't know if they're souls or reapers. I just know they're in pain. We have to free them."

"We will, but we have to take care of Anubis first. Once he's dead, then we can drain the well and release the spirits. With any hope the energy that was collected will be returned. I overheard them talking. He's going to use their power and break out. If he does, then all will be lost. He will bring death to the world. That's what he wants. He wants to rule everyone and annihilate the entire human race. Go. I believe in you."

I went behind him into the dark and suffocating passageway. Shadows moved off the wall and wrapped around me. Their tethers latched onto me and burned the way that the fabric of my robe would do to an enemy. This whole place was woven and made of death. *Is this the origin of where it all came from?* There had to be more to this whole story than what I was getting from Azrael. The shadows burned along any exposed skin. I gathered my strength and willed myself alive. When my skin warmed and my heart beat, the shadows released me. I pulled back my hood and took a risk. I banished the cloak so I was nothing more than a living soul among the dead. Once I became alive, the shadows vanished. The darkness and heavy atmosphere retreated. Torches ignited as I walked by. Cobwebs filled the staircase. The spiders were the size of my fist. Small sand drifts lined the sandstone steps. I touched the stone, and the vibrations I got from it were full of death and sorrow. I got a flash of someone being pushed down the steps and their neck snapping at an odd angle. Another shadow glided over the entrance at the top of the stairs. I waited in the doorway. A cold tremor passed over me. The shadow stopped. It couldn't see me. Being alive worked to my advantage.

At least for now.

I drew in another breath and stifled a cough from the dust. I grabbed one of the torches. A breeze passed by my left cheek when I went into the hallway. The corridor to the right had stagnant air. I was flying blind on this one. Being human didn't allow me to see half of what I could as a reaper. I closed my eyes, reached out, and connected with my guides. Their warmth filled me and allowed me to have the second sight to gaze at the other world.

When I opened my eyes, the guards that patrolled this place were visible. I followed the guards a ways and moved away from the dungeon area. In one room vast columns carved with hieroglyphs and sketchings of gods filled the room. Paint came off on my fingers when I touched them. Most of it was intact as though age hadn't touched it. I wasn't sure exactly where we were, but it didn't feel like the graveyard. Yet it wasn't all the way into the real world. A limbo. I could understand why Anubis would want to break out. *Maybe he's already brought them closer to the real world. I can't let Anubis out to bring death to the rest of the world.* I stretched out my senses and felt an enormous amount of energy emanating from down the passage. The sound of dead scarabs crunched underneath my feet as I walked on them. Each echoed through the hall. Someone would hear me, but no one sprang out to grab me.

At closer inspection of one column, the scene of an angel held a scythe decorated it. When I touched the column, I was hit with the image of people bowing down before this great being. A name flashed in my mind.

Gabriel.

Azrael said he was the first one to rule over Death. On the next column Gabriel had bodies underneath him. Smaller winged guides helped each body toward a great light. I touched that painting and was barraged with images of angels taking the souls of the dead toward the hereafter. The next column showed another angel bowing down before Gabriel. His arms were up. Gabriel presented him with the scythe. He had long dark hair, was dark skinned and was dressed in a black robe instead of a white. In the transition the angels escorting the dead were also clad in black. It didn't exactly say what Anubis had been before. *Maybe he was a priest. Maybe he was something more, and that's the reason why he was lifted above.*

When I touched the next pillar, it wasn't like the other images. It was from my perspective. I stood before a half-constructed pyramid. I looked around and saw the same man who I had seen in the other vision when he was getting the scythe. He smiled at me and took my hand. A strong rush of feelings overtook me. I pulled my hand away. The energy me left me reeling. I dropped the torch and hit another column behind me. The echo of it crashed through the empty hall, and I knew someone heard me.

A cold breeze whisked by me and a hulking presence hovered. I wasn't about to shift my focus and look back into the threshold of death to be sure. Instead I glanced at the last column. Anubis with the jackal head and the body of a man was etched into the stone. Gone were his wings. Jackals lead the souls. The next scene showed mummies replaced the souls. Anubis's eyes held a meanness I couldn't place. I placed my hand on the next column.

My stomach turned. The man desecrated the dead that he had once mummified. A deep hurt ate him up on the inside that left his heart dead. *What made you so cold and twisted?* The torch flickered. Something scurried in the darkness. As long as I remained alive, I was safe. I focused on trying to have my heart beat, but deep within me I sensed the tug of the well. The trapped souls called to me. The flashes from touching the columns lingered, and I had to sort them out.

The torch went out. Once the darkness took over, a touch of death came upon me again. My guides told me to get up slowly and follow the energy. It led me into the main room. In the center was a bluish-purple illumination emanating from the pit. I walked to the edge before I realized it. A loose brick wobbled underneath my foot. I snapped back to reality. The matter inside the well was neither liquid nor solid.

"It's beautiful, isn't it?" A cool voice said behind me. It reminded me of Mastema's, but something about it was much more familiar.

I stiffened but didn't turn around. "It's a pretty thing if you didn't know exactly what you're looking at."

"And you know what that is?"

"You know I do."

"Are you ready to kill me, or try to at least?"

I turned to Anubis. The torches snapped to life. The tomb was opulent. All the walls were gold. The hall was lined with jackals all laying on pedestals. At the end of the row was a large gold throne. To the right of the throne stood a large sarcophagus. On the left side of the throne sat the sphinx. Even alive I sensed the power of the creature. It waited for me to make a move against Anubis as were the other jackals. Three of the statues were smashed and three more remained. All dark eyes of the creatures were on me. To the right of the throne was a small throne for Anubis' queen.

The walls of the tomb told the story more clearly than the columns did. I tried to keep my gaze away from him. I walked over to the wall and looked at the scenes. One of them seemed familiar. A woman and a man watched the building of a pyramid. I ran my fingers over the couple and something stirred within me. Pressure pushed against my thoughts like something wanted to be opened. I found myself within the scene. The acrid scent of the dust filled my nose. The warmth of the sun caressed my flesh. The songs of the slaves raising the stones echoed in my ears. A hand slipped around my waist. When I looked over I saw Anubis. His eyes bright and happy.

The weight built within my mind. I tried to push it aside and focus on the task before me. But the pressure gave me a headache. Another scene popped in my mind. Anubis lay beside me. He fed me grapes and chuckled as we both joked. He kissed me and his other hand slid over my round belly. A foot pressed out of the skin on my stomach from the child I carried. We both laughed and were happy from the expected blessing to come.

Tears glided down my cheeks as emotions overwhelmed

me. *This isn't happening. It can't be what I think it is.* I wiped my cheeks and gathered my composure. The weight remained on my mind. Whatever was behind it was nearly ready to burst.

"You never answered my question. Are you going to *try* and kill me? That *is* your job. That's the reason Azrael sent you here and why I haven't sensed you. You're something a little different. His secret weapon and his undoing."

"I'm here…" But I couldn't bring myself to say anything else. My hand slid over my stomach as I could feel the echo of the life within me.

"I've waited a long time for you. You're the culmination of all the keys falling into place and the right doors opening. And you're right where I want you. Now there's one thing left to do to release me from this purgatory."

I pressed my fingernails into my palm. The pain helped to cut me from the visions invading my mind. I turned from the painting and studied the man before me. His skin was dark, not black, tinted with a little red and tan depending on how the light hit his flesh. Anubis was lean, but he was muscular. A white kilt wrapped around his waist. A gold necklace hung around his neck with the Eye of Horus pendent resting over his heart. Sharp cheekbones accentuated his cheeks and a thin nose. His eyes were dark and filled with wisdom and sorrow. His hair was braided and tinkled with gold ankhs, scarabs, and other ornaments when he moved his head. He wore sandals that barely covered his feet. As my gaze settled back on his face, the amused smile turned into a frown.

"What else do you need from me to release you?" I tried to ignore more of the fuzzy memories forming in my mind. They felt like bubbles coming to the surface, but they weren't ready to pop. The memories shouldn't be there. As a reaper I had access to all of my past life memories. Unless someone had deliberately kept them from me.

"You're making this too easy." He lunged and shoved me backwards.

I lost my footing and felt myself falling. Blue tendrils of energy wrapped around me. It was a peaceful feeling at first. Like I could drift away and dream as they drew me into the well. Then the agony started. Every place where the tentacles touched it was like a fishhook shoved into my pores and ripped out over and over again. Everything was blue. The shrieking souls of those around me filled my ears. I couldn't help them. We all were being tortured. Every part of me was being pulled away a little at a time. I was in hell.

And then the pain ceased.

CHAPTER TWELVE

I opened my eyes again. Anubis's dark gaze was filled with confusion. His arms were around me. It felt right to be in them. The devil said some things were never truly over even if I thought they were. Azrael said we couldn't escape our fate. This wasn't right, and yet it was. I tried to make sense of it all. Anubis had pushed me into the well, and now I was in his arms and his malice had drained away. What in the world was going on?

I reached up and tried to touch his cheek, but he flinched. The confusion returned to his eyes. I raised my hand to his cheek. This time he didn't shy away. Once I did, the bubbles inside of my mind popped. Th past life I'd been missing rushed back and filled a hole in my soul I didn't know I had. His name, his true name, sat on my lips. It came out in a language long dead.

"Anapa," I whispered. "Fate is so cruel."

"Anput." Tears lined his eyes as he pressed his lips to mine.

He tasted like dry parchment and jasmine and cedar. I returned the kiss until he shook his head and pulled away. Although being with him felt right, another's image flashed in my mind. Than. He was my soul mate. The man I loved and the one who Anubis had tortured. Yet, my hidden lifetime with Anubis played in my mind. I had loved him. Part of me still did.

"We can't change our fate no matter how much we fight it." I sat up slowly and found him leaning against a sarcophagus. The aroma of spices, old linen, and the stench of death filled the tomb. I ran my hand over the edge of the stone coffin. It was inlaid with gold and lapis made from the same black material as my weapons. His screams at what they had done to him erupted in my mind. They mummified him alive, pulled out his organs, and embalmed him until he was nothing more than a husk and wrapped in bindings. And he remained conscious.

I experienced the trauma he went through, and all the while he screamed out for me. He was left to stew, and it drove him insane. He fell into a slumber, and then he was awoken by...but before I could see that he pulled my hand away.

"You're her. Somewhere inside, you're my beloved wife. After all that was done to her. And Azrael sends you to me."

The memories of my demise as his wife washed over me. I struggled as I was ripped from his arms. He might have been a god, but I had been human. A priestess of Anubis that he had fallen in love with. Ours was a forbidden love. I gave birth to a daughter with him. The other gods discovered I was human. The other death gods pulled me away from him. That was when he started to go a little crazy. Anubis desired to keep me with him. My soul had already departed my body, but I was the first one he embalmed and mummified.

"I didn't know."

"Apparently." He leaned against the throne. A low growl came from the platform next to him. Anubis followed my gaze.

"Master, remember what she's needed for," the sphinx

snarled.

"Quiet!" Anubis snapped. A flicker of his human façade melted away, revealing a jackal head underneath. I touched his arm, and he focused back on me. I threaded my fingers through his. It returned his human persona.

"Tell me what happened?" I entreated him.

"They tore you from my arms. What else was I supposed to do? The other gods, they've all had relationships with humans. They saw our daughter as an abomination because of who she was. They saw me sympathizing with humans and not doing my job. I wanted to keep you, to make you one of the jackals, one of the reapers, as you call them now. They started out as angels under Gabriel. They became the jackals under me, or whatever the other gods needed them to be. Then Azrael was chosen over all. He didn't deserve it. That lowlife vampire was raised up. I was going to show them all and get you back. You were going to rule at my side. We were going to take over the world and make the humans pay. The other death gods said I'd gone insane. They said I couldn't bring you back because you'd already been through too many incarnations to be with me." He ran his fingers down my cheek. "They locked you away and said I'd never find you again. I swore they would all pay for what they did to you. They mutilated your body and pulled you apart. It was all I could do to save your organs and put them in the jars. Everything else of you I wrapped in linen and made sure your body was protected." He waved his hand and another sarcophagus appeared along the wall behind his, standing upright. It was painted to look like a woman, that any queen would be interred in. He moved the lid away revealing a mummy inside.

Something tugged inside of me as part of me remembered this was the flesh I had come from.

"I asked some of the jackals where you had incarnated into next. If I could find just one lifetime, I could get the trace of your soul energy. From there I could track you down no matter what human flesh you wore. When they wouldn't tell me, I started collecting souls so I could have the power to resurrect you. They kept you from me." He stroked the mummy's face.

"The columns outside showed you were once an angel when Gabriel gave you the scythe. How is it you became a Death god?" I asked.

"Humans got so much of the mythology wrong. I was an angel, but when I took over things changed. We were closer to humans, but not close enough to the heavens as we once were. We lesser angels became death gods. We became something else, something more, depending on what humans believed in. Soon we were shaped by death and our duties, and nothing could change that fact. They said I went mad, but I knew what I was doing all of the time." He stopped and glanced at me. The look of utter loss on his face made my heart break. "I couldn't get you back."

"So you became a god, I was taken from you, and you were locked up. Why are you doing this now, Anapa?" My love lingered within my soul, but it was fading as if I was looking at photographs of my life from before. I could connect with the love, but my heart was set on Than. *He* was my soul mate.

Anubis pulled his gaze away from the mummy and looked back at me. He took my hands in his. He studied me for a long time before placing a hand over my heart. "Your heart beats as though you were alive, and yet I sense the death in you. The prophecy was true. It's because of you that I've been given the chance to be free. My loyal servants have given me the chance to escape this hell. What do I do with you? Azrael's secret weapon.

Someone who is dead and not completely alive. You could rule over this reality and all worlds. You're stronger than all of them. You're something completely new with death and life in your hands. You can walk both sides if you wished it. Even just those few minutes in the well have altered you even more. You could be at my side, but then I wouldn't be able to break out of here and take my rightful place in the hierarchy of things. Azrael belongs back in hell with Mastema. He's a filthy demon."

What he said doesn't make any sense. I'm a reaper no matter what Azrael's done to me. "He's my boss. He's been good to me. I enjoy my life. I love being a reaper and still being alive to help people. Don't you remember what it was like? You can't corrupt the dead. Your time has passed, Anapa. Maybe we can work something out, and you can still be free. I don't want to hurt you. I don't want Azrael to hurt you. We're reapers."

He closed his eyes and drew in a long breath. "Would you spend the rest of eternity with me? We could get to know one another again. I could get to know who you've become."

"If only it were that easy. There's someone else. He's the one I'm supposed to be with. I'm not saying that I don't still feel something for you, because that's there. Can you share me with another?"

Anubis glared at me. I didn't have to see his eyes flash golden to know he was pissed. "No. I never was very good at sharing you. Even with our daughter. I guess it's settled. You truly are dead." He pulled me into him to kiss me once more.

It was a long and hard kiss that bruised my lips. It poured all of his feelings into me. I sensed the loneliness and the longing and the need for revenge. I wrapped my arms around his neck. I didn't want to believe he would hurt me. I didn't want to believe he was a monster behind all of the death and sorrow. I wanted to believe he was the husband I remembered from the past. Underneath it all, he was different. I returned the kiss with the same fervor before he pulled away.

"Don't do this."

"I don't have another choice. Goodbye, Anput." I heard the growl in his voice.

He thrust me away from him. His head became that of a jackal only he was not fully reconstructed. Half of his face was flesh and the other part was mummified. His hands were claws. And jagged yellow teeth protruded over his lips. I dropped the pretense of being alive. Warmth drained from my body. My heart stopped. The texture of the world around me changed. Gone were the cobwebs and the stone walls. Gone were the torches and the innocent looking stone jackals and the stone sphinx. Instead I saw the dark animal who had come to the house and was telling me I only had one chance. Well here was my last chance, and he was going to try and put me back into the well.

"Don't make me do this." I held the scythe as the jackals snarled around me.

Anubis grinned. "You really think you can fend me off with that little stick?" He waved his hand, and the scythe reappeared in his clutches. "This is the true weapon of death."

He cracked it in half as if it were kindling. A larger eight feet tall scythe came in his hand. The curved blade was over four feet long and deadly. Anubis swung it with an ease of any reaper. The jackals jumped off the pedestals and circled us. The sphinx shored up the circle leaving me standing before Anubis. A sliver of fear stabbed my heart. He would have the final key to break him out of this realm. The slight click clack of tiny feet as hordes of scarabs surrounded us on all sides made me shiver. One was a foot long. It crawled up Anubis's body until it rested on his shoulder. Its antenna wiggled against his neck. I couldn't help but be disturbed by it. I suppressed a shiver and thought about what Than had gone through. When I thought of him, my resolve tightened. It didn't matter what had happened in a past life. If there was one thing I was going to do, it was get my revenge. Maybe my beloved wasn't dead. I had to be sure.

"Fine, you're going to kill me or use my soul, so that you can break out of here. Before you do, don't you think you can do me one favor, considering our history?"

"A dying wish."

"You could say that. Will you grant it no matter what I ask?"

"I give you my word."

"Free Than. Give him back his soul and his power." I held my breath that my hunch was correct.

"This is the one that you love?"

"Yes."

"We need him, my lord," the sphinx grumbled.

"Quiet," he snapped.

He brought the scythe to my throat. I waited for the swipe of the blade, but it never came. Anubis waved his other hand. A skeletal, shrunken figure appeared before me. Its shredded wings dragged along on the ground. The only thing still lively about him was his eyes. He reached toward me.

I reached toward him. "Than."

"Kill me," he gasped.

"No," Anubis chuckled. "It's so much more fun seeing you this way. Torturing you was exquisite. It got her here."

"You promised," I reminded Anubis.

He grinned. "You want him more than me, Anput?"

"He's the other half of my soul, Anapa. I'll go willingly into the well, but—"

"No," Than rasped. "Kerstin, no!"

"Done." He snapped his fingers. A tentacle of blue-white light speared Than in the center of the chest. A purple glow emanated around him and lifted him off the ground. His wings filled out and became the grand things they once were. The rest of him plumped, and the spear returned into the well, leaving him whole. Anubis released the scythe, and I went over to Than. He took me in his arms and kissed me. Feeling him whole and knowing he would be okay was what motivated me.

"He's free as requested and won't be touched. Now do as you said, beloved."

Than grabbed my arm. "Don't. We can find another way."

I touched his face, feeling the softness of his skin once more. "There isn't another way. Find a way to stop him."

I vanished the reaper attire and stood before Anubis. He snapped his fingers once more. A white linen dress wrapped around my body. My wrists were covered with gold bracelets and a cuff for each arm carved with the figures of death. I ran my fingers over them and remembered when he had given them to me to mark me for his wife. He was still in there somewhere, but Anubis had said his goodbyes.

The scarabs parted and let me pass. The energy in the well frothed. A large tentacle came out and stopped right before it enveloped me. Everything froze. Dark laughter echoed in the hall around me. Mastema leaned against the wall.

"What do you want?"

"Are you really going to accept your destiny? Once that arm touches you, you won't come out of the Well of Souls. It's bad enough you've been in there once. The lasting effects of it can be quite devastating."

"What do you care, Mastema? I've accepted my fate. If I go

into the well, Than goes free. He'll find a way to return Anubis to his coffin. I trust him. Azrael will escape, and they'll take care of it. Once they defeat him, then they can get me from the well."

Mastema strutted over, showing off his tight hugging leather pants and no shirt. He batted the tentacle away from me, and an annoyed look crossed his face. "Do you want to know what's going to happen with the world once Anubis sets foot in it?"

"You're going to show me whether I ask you to or not."

"True."

He waved his arm, and the golden wall before me changed. We stood in the middle of a city. Flames shot out of the windows and people screamed. Dead bodies littered the streets. The dried husks of scarabs were strewn about. Jackals ran free attacking people. Some people were infested with the scarabs, eating their way out from the inside. Smoke and ash darkened the sky. Souls lingered by their bodies or wandered aimlessly because no one guided them over to the other side. Winged creatures fought the jackals. Reapers appeared with scythes and cut down the angels and stole their power. Anubis's laughter rang out above the din. Than stood by his side with a scythe in hand.

A woman ran by them unaware.

"Take her," Anubis commanded.

Than gave him a slight nod. He stretched out his hand. The black threads of his robe shot out and wrapped around her. They burned her when they touched her flesh. She screamed and fell to the ground. Her face turned my stomach. The more she squirmed, the more entangled in the black web of his cloak she became until everything except her head was encompassed. He knelt before her.

"Please don't hurt me."

He gave her a cruel laugh. "Too late for begging." He plunged his hand into the center of her chest and withdrew a pulsating blue, white orb with small tendrils anchored into her skin. The small threads broke apart from her body when he tugged on it. Her soul struggled to stay within her body because it wasn't her time yet. Her cries ceased. He knelt before Anubis and held up the soul.

"My lord, for you."

Anubis patted his head. "Good boy. You're such a good soldier. It was good of Kerstin to give herself over to me, wasn't it?"

I waited for Than to have some reaction to my name. His face and his eyes didn't waiver. He was dead inside. He no longer had a soul. He was an angel once more and lost every shred of humanity he ever had. "Yes."

Than rose and stared blankly at a jackal ripping into the woman's flesh. Anubis petted the jackal closest to him. "What did you see in her? Did you ever even love her?"

"She was a mere distraction. She meant nothing to me. How could I love her when she is a perversion to what we are? True death cannot be alive."

A rush of sadness washed over me. I turned away from the apocalyptic scene and swallowed my sadness. This couldn't happen to Than. I couldn't let the world fall to ruin because of a choice I made. I had to do something about it. Or maybe this was all in Mastema's plan. "This is all some kind of trick. Showing me this so I'll give in to you and accept the favor you owe me. Get the hell out of here and leave me alone."

He wagged his finger. "But I'm not going to leave you alone. I'm not going to let you go. You should've realized that by now. What you see here is not just the future for one world, but for all worlds. All times. All planes that death touches. Ask your guides if you don't believe me."

"Why? Why me? What you showed me was a lie. That's what you are, the Prince of Lies. You're evil." I turned away from him. The beauty of the devil was a little overwhelming considering everything that was going on. I couldn't look into those eyes of his without feeling something inside of me slipping away and falling under his power. He said to ask my guides, but part of me knew that if I did, I would hear the same truth from them.

"It's a true outcome of the future if you step into the well. You'll suffer forever in a hell of your own making. Ask your guides. For the reason of why you, well that's a little more complicated than I can explain right now. I'm running out of time in this reality. I only have so much power here before Anubis will detect why time has stopped. But as I said, I can offer you a way out of this and a way to defeat him."

"How can I trust you? You set this all up with Anubis in the beginning. You started all of this with him back when he ruled over the dead and he was worshipped in Egypt as a god."

The devil's eyes narrowed and darkness came into his gaze. "I did what I had to do in the beginning because of the way that things were going. We were friends when he was still an angel. Anubis never saw me as a fallen creature. Who do you think kept the other death gods from you for so long so you could have your happy life and your daughter? I did everything I could so you could remain together. I didn't utter the prophecy that said you'd come again, and it would spell the doom of the planet. Whether you believe it or not, I want Earth in all its different realities to thrive. I don't want it to die. Blame it on the souls that I collect or the influence that I have. Don't think that I don't care. I didn't bind your memories. I kept tabs on Anubis, and assisted the other gods in binding him. I didn't stir the other gods."

"Then who was it? Who awoke him and bound my memories?" My head spun even more. The devil was telling me he was Anubis's friend and he wanted the world to continue. Who bound my memories so I wouldn't remember this? What is this prophecy he's talking about? "It's all a bunch of bullshit. You want to confuse me more."

"If I wanted to confuse, would I reveal the future when I don't directly interact with the real world?"

"What about using the serial killer last year and trying to get me to open the door so that Anubis could be free?"

Mastema grabbed my shoulders. His nails pierced my flesh. I didn't react from the pain and stared right back at him. I knew better than to show fear. "It was another agenda. Another time. I had my reasons. I didn't know what he was planning to do. If I thought he was going to take over the world and make it into his own playground, I wouldn't have gotten involved. I'm for him dethroning Azrael and changing around the current regime. He's not the same person, angel, man, god, whatever you want to call him from the last time I saw him. It all started when he lost you and couldn't reconnect your soul with your body. It was all he talked about for a long time. Look, I know you killed two of the gods who were meant to bring you to him, but there are others hiding in plain sight. They are dangerous. If this all goes south for them, then they'll come after you. I can offer you protection."

"Really? Why would I want protection from you after everything you've done to me? I—" Mastema cut me off when he planted his lips on mine.

In that split second, I forgot everything I was going to say and was caught up in the lust that swept through me. I couldn't help but return the kiss. I tried to push him once I regained my composure. He swiped his tongue over my lips. A small moan crept up my throat. All I wanted was a bed to take out my frustrations on. Sex with him would be the ultimate indulgence, but it wouldn't go right to my thighs like chocolate or cheesecake would. It would go to my soul. I touched his tongue with mine as he pulled me closer and molded his body to mine. Everything in me responded to this overwhelming yearning building up inside of me. Mastema pulled away, panting.

"You have no idea how much you make me want you. Only a few women have ever done that, and you still deny me. Most would've caved and said yes to me now."

"Maybe that's why you want me. You enjoy the chase. If I ever said yes to you, really said yes, then you wouldn't want me anymore."

He pushed a strand of hair from my cheek. "That's not true. There's just something about you. It's like a beacon that draws me to you. Enough of this game. We have very little time left. I can give you a way out of this."

"Does that include helping to free Azrael?"

Mastema gritted his teeth. "Yes."

"What's your offer?" *I can at least hear him out. I'm standing on death's door. If the world is going to burn, then I have a minute to hear his proposal.*

"You will become mine. Wholly in body and—"

"Don't say soul. Cause that's never going to happen."

He grunted. A few flames curled around his nostrils. "Fine. You'll be mine. You'll be my grim reaper. You will collect souls for me without question."

Reapers were supposed to be neutral. "What about Than? Do you expect me to reside in hell with you where you can ravage me over and over again? What about having free will?"

"I won't harm your lover nor will I lift a finger against

Azrael. It's been forbidden anyway for me. As to your free will and residing in hell, I'll allow you to keep your life as you have it now, whatever the arrangement is with Azrael being the hybrid you are. However, I will have full access to you wherever you are and you will have access to hell. I'll send my agents to you if need be."

"What about the favor you owe me?"

"It comes off the table unless you do something for me that I deem worthy."

Something scuttled closer, and the tentacle wiggled. His power waned over stopping time. The fate of my soul. The fate of the world, and not to mention the rest of the universe hung in the balance. *Is my happiness and sanity worth sacrificing everything?* That answer was easy. No. It wasn't. There's no other way around this. I have to do the right thing this time. Unlike where I jumped into a quick decision about Death's Dance as Lissandra. *Than won't ever forgive me for this. I have to take the chance I might lose him to save him.* The idea hurt my heart, but time ticked down. Did I sacrifice myself and let the world burn for him to become an unfeeling angel and Anubis' whipping boy? Or did I give myself over to the devil and save everything? "Fine. But don't expect me to sign anything or that this is an invitation to get into my pants."

The triumph in his eyes made his smile even more wicked. "Good. Good. We can hammer out the details when this is all over."

"Fine. Make sure Azrael's free. What do I do about Anubis?"

The devil waved his hand and a sickle appeared in it. It looked like the same one I had still hidden within my robe. "That's the same one, isn't it?"

"The very same one, but it's the first weapon Anubis ever had. I fashioned it for him, so he could use it to separate souls from their bodies. It will do as much damage as the scythe he has. Once time starts back again, summon your robe. It will protect you. Use the claw from the sphinx. It will do as much damage on him as it did on those reapers. It's poisonous for anything death related. You'll have to move fast. I can only give you one good blast to clear a path. Then I'll get Azrael. Understand?"

I gripped the sickle. Lucifer stood behind me. He placed his hands on my shoulders. I tried not to flinch, but the thought of him touching me made it worse because of what I agreed to. What will Than say? What will Azrael say? The air around us stirred. The power of the well reached to me, but Mastema protected me from the tendrils. A blast of heat surrounded me. I glimpsed his wings as they encompassed the room. With one great flash of fire the scarabs were crispy critters and the jackals whimpered as the flames washed over them. Once the heat dissipated, Mastema vanished as well.

I held up the sickle.

"Where did you get that?" Anubis asked. "Only one other possessed that weapon."

"Then you know where I got it." The coldness of death encompassed my being along with something else, a touch of warmth. The devil's hold on me. *How am I going to get myself out of this one?*

"Mastema."

I shoved my hand into the pocket of my robe and pulled out the sphinx claw. The end of it was wrapped so I could hold it. I ran at Anubis. He laughed and swung the scythe at me. I ducked so the blade went over my head. The whoosh of the air stirred my hair. At the same time he swung, I jabbed at him with the sphinx claw. I caught his fleshy bicep. He spun around and faced me. The tip of the scythe had sliced my arm. He yanked out the talon and threw it across the tomb.

He stopped when the sphinx growled behind me.

"Did you really think you and Mastema could turn my beasts against me?" Anubis took a step toward me.

I stepped back. The burn of the wound radiated up my arm, but I didn't drop the sickle. The power of the well reached for me.

"Come to me," it whispered to my mind.

"You hear the sound of the well calling you back to it," Anubis said right by my ear.

I jumped when I felt his hands on my shoulders. He wasn't pushing me forward. "Yes."

All my tension drained away as he turned me around to face the well. The bluish light from the well surrounded the sphinx. It was almost beautiful. I saw the black skin of his muzzle and the sleek black hair that was his fur. He was a gigantic beast. His claws left scars in the limestone floor. Anubis ran his fingers down my cheek. I could feel the sharpness of his claws and the softness of his pelt. I tried to break out of the haze I was in, but I was helpless.

A bluish tendril rose out of the well. It danced back and forth trying to hypnotize me. Soft voices in the well called, wanted me to rejoin them.

"Come now, Anput. There will be no pain this time. I promise. Look over there."

I followed his gaze and saw the wall fade away behind the well until it was the heavy wall of fog. It folded away and revealed a window into the regular world. I didn't know where I was looking at, but it was a city like any other with people walking by. It reminded me of the vision that Mastema had shown me with Anubis taking over the world. "Where does that go?"

"It leads to the real world. From your sacrifice, I can enter the world and let them know who and what death truly is. No more hiding in the shadows. No more letting them know that death is a peaceful thing. All those souls will go into the well. Reapers will bring them here. The one who rules over us and Mastema will no longer take the power of the souls. They will bow down to me. Just let yourself go into the well."

"No. You know I can't do that. Anapa, please." I didn't have the strength to look away from the blue snake trying to lure me. It was a struggle to think. "Somewhere inside of you, I know you still love me. I know that you don't want to do this. What if I stay with you?"

"We've already been through that. You have another man who you love more than life itself. Now he's abandoned you. I can understand why because you made a deal with the devil. Look where it got you." He shoved me toward the tentacle. My legs remained locked. Heat spiked along my spine as the power of hell entered me. Mastema took control of my body. He wasn't going to let his investment go to waste. My hand tightened on the sickle. I turned and swung. Anubis ducked out of the way. The sphinx jumped between us.

"I told you that you had one chance to make the right decision. Now you die, or I'll push you into that well. My lord will be free."

"I don't think so." Azrael appeared next to me with his scythe. "Kerstin, I believe this is my fight. I should have done this ages ago."

I nodded.

"You're mine," Azrael said to the sphinx. The jackals snarled as if they were the being fought off by someone.

I brought the sickle up before Anubis. "I won't go into the well. I won't let you destroy the world. But I don't want to hurt you." A tear trickled down my cheek.

"Oh really?"

"You know I don't want this. I won't let you tear the souls apart either. We're meant to bring them into the other realms and nothing more."

"You sound like Azrael. You have become just like him."

"Yes. I have. I might have been the product of some prophecy come to unlock you from this tomb, but it will not come to pass."

Behind me the sphinx shrieked, and he fell silent. Anubis didn't flinch when his pet died. He screamed and came at me with the scythe. I stumbled backward and swung at him with the sickle. My robe sensed the danger and snagged his leg. He tried to pull away, but couldn't, it was stronger than steel cable.

"Finally figured out how to use your robe. You have to know how to win their trust. Have you done that?" Anubis asked.

He was stalling. He tried to lift the scythe again, but it nearly fell from his grip. The poison from the sphinx talon was working on him. "I don't think it matters."

"I think she's right, Anubis." Azrael's scythe dripped black blood. Than stood behind him.

The jackal god tried to hold his scythe. The threads on my robe broke. Anubis tried to strike at me again, but the weapon dropped from his hand. He sunk down to the floor before me, and the jackal persona faded, revealing only the man.

Black vines of the poison crept up his shoulder. Pain shadowed his eyes. "Anput," he whispered.

Than pressed the scythe to Anubis's throat. "Get up and face your judgment. For what you've done to her and these reapers."

Anubis laughed. "You really think I care about what's been done to the other reapers? Do think that the likes of you and this half-breed monster can rule over death any better than I have?

You who know nothing, a petty angel who has forgotten what heaven was like."

"I haven't forgotten what it was like. I remember every little detail, but there's more to the world than Heaven," Than countered.

"Anubis, it's not going to work. You won't take over the world." Azrael picked up the large scythe, the symbol of his office. "Get up. It's time to put you back in your sarcophagus. Free all those in your well."

"Why would I do you any favors? Those loyal to me will keep on trying to break me out. Even if you want to punish them, you have to find them." Anubis spat and nearly toppled over.

"Do as he says." Than butted him with the end of the scythe.

Anubis laughed and spit out a mouthful of blood. "Or what? Are you going to kill me now?"

I sank down next to Anubis. I drew him into my arms and heard the rattling in his lungs as he drew breath. He was starting to get cold and truly dying. "Stop this. Please. Anapa, release the souls. You can't go on like this. Azrael can heal you, but you have to let the souls free."

He threaded his fingers through mine and brought our combined hands to his lips. "There's no use. I'm already rotting away. What's the use if you're not here with me."

"What does he mean by that?" Than asked.

"Don't worry about it now, Than. Drain the well, my love."

"A dying petition. Always the demanding one who kept me in check. I have one last request for you."

"What's that?" I asked.

"Kiss me once more before I go."

I pressed my mouth to his, feeling those once soft lips becoming thin and leathery. I pulled away. His skin was withering.

Anubis was no longer the crazed monster who wanted to take over the world, just a fallen, dying man.

"Thank you, beloved. How I missed seeing you." He pulled the Eye of Horus from his neck and pressed it into my hand. Anubis waved his other hand and said a few words in ancient Egyptian. The well exploded. A great pillar of energy hit the ceiling followed by the shrill screams of trapped souls. The lights of their souls flew away. I prayed some returned to the reapers in the cells below.

Energy settled over. The part of me in the well clicked back into place. My tears fell upon his shrunken skin, and his flesh drank up the moisture. "Stay strong. Maybe one day I'll see you again."

I glanced up at Azrael. "Can you heal him?"

He sighed.

"No," Anubis wheezed. "Put me back in the sarcophagus. Let me rest."

Azrael nodded. He slipped his arm underneath Anubis's shoulder and helped me walk him back over to the sarcophagus. He was a bag of bones that rattled around within his flesh. Than even helped. We put him back into the coffin and moved the lid on top of it. I touched his face one last time. Anubis flashed me a smile before the darkness of the coffin took him.

That chapter of my life was over, sealed away as my memories once were.

CHAPTER THIRTEEN

I slid down the sarcophagus to the floor. Memories of my life with Anubis played in my mind. It shouldn't have been this way. Than sat next to me and wrapped his arm around me. I leaned my head on his shoulder. Him being safe lifted my heart. I couldn't enjoy it because the deal I made with Mastema played in my thoughts. How am I going to tell him?

"What happened?" Than asked.

"How about we get Kerstin home, and then we can all discuss it?" Azrael suggested.

He handed me the sickle and held out his hand so I could get up. Than kept his arm around my waist as he whisked me away from the tombs. I wasn't exactly sure where we landed. When I looked up, we were back at Azrael's home. Although something about it didn't look right. We were back in the kitchen. A streak of blood ran across the tile floor and led into the hallway as though someone had been dragged. The table was toppled over and one of the legs askew. Three of the chairs were shattered into small pieces.

"Brenna," Azrael called.

I disconnected with Than and shoved the Eye of Horus into my pocket. "Doni? Angela?" I yelled.

I listened but didn't hear them answer me. I followed the blood trail into the living room. Angela was sprawled out on the floor. Her throat was ripped out. Gnaw marks marred her leg and her stomach. I sank down beside her. "No. No. No."

Azrael came down the stairs in a rush. "Brenna's gone. So is Doni."

"Where could they have gone?" Than asked.

"I have no idea. From the looks of it a jackal or the sphinx got her." I moved my hands over her eyes and closed them. "I'm so sorry. I thought you'd be safe here."

"There has to be something for us to know where they were taken," Than said.

Azrael closed his eyes and concentrated. "I can't sense her. That hasn't happened in a long time. Something has to be really wrong. She would have defended Doni. Who would have taken her? Anubis is back in his sarcophagus. He's too weak to do anything."

"He said there were others who were loyal to him. I don't know who they are, but I might have a way to find them both," I said to him.

"Anything. Please."

"You're not going to like it." I didn't want to reveal it to them, but I wasn't about to leave my friends to a rogue death god. "Mastema," I called out.

The devil appeared in a flash of fire, all pomp and circumstance. "You rang?"

"Brenna is missing and Azrael doesn't know where she is. So is one of my friends that I brought here for safe keeping. The other is dead. I thought you might know where she is."

"Kerstin, what did you do?" Than asked.

The deal had been struck. "I'm sorry. It was the only way to free you and Azrael and not start world annihilation."

The veins popped in my boss's forehead. "Hello, brother. Can you help us or not?"

"I'm not sure. Brenna is such a delectable woman. It's too bad you lost her."

"We don't have time for a pissing contest. Will you help me or not?" I asked the devil.

He smiled. "I'll help you, but only for a kiss."

Than jumped between us. "Over my dead body, you will."

Mastema winked at me. "That can easily happen, reaper, but I don't think you want to anger your beloved right now."

I put a hand on Than's chest and pushed him a way. "It's fine. We'll deal with it later." I kissed the devil on the cheek. "Satisfied?"

"Not really? You know what I want." Mastema said.

He slipped his arm around my waist and pulled me close. He pressed his lips around mine and kissed me with an over-the-top show to piss off Than. I returned the kiss, but this time I wasn't overwhelmed with the lust I had been before. Pledging myself to him must have taken care of that aspect of his charm. He released me and smiled at his conquest. I went to Than, but he wouldn't come near me, and that nearly broke my heart.

"I did what you asked. Now, where is she?" I demanded.

Lucifer said something with a couple of clicks within the string of hissing syllables. A small black imp about two feet tall appeared next to him with red eyes. Its spaded tail was longer than its body. One red horn jutted from the center of its forehead. It listened and then nodded. "He'll be right back."

"You trust an imp?" Azrael asked.

"He's my creation. Of course, I do. Then again, you're my

creation as well, Azrael, but there is too much water under that bridge. I'll always be able to find those who are bound to me or have my blood in their veins. For future reference if you ever lose Brenna again."

"You're a son of a bitch," Azrael muttered.

"Of course, I am. I thought that was established a long time ago." A small pop echoed in the living room, and the imp appeared next to the devil again. He said something and then vanished. "Brenna is with Anubis's mother. You should be able to track her from that information. Follow the imp. He'll lead you there. Do you think you can handle it from here? Kerstin, I expect to see you soon."

"Fuck off," I snapped.

Mastema chuckled and faded away, leaving two burning footprints in the wooden floor. A sharp snap went across my cheek and turned my head from the force. I rubbed my skin from the slap across my jaw.

"How could you?" Than spat.

"I didn't have a choice. I told you that. I couldn't let you die or go on existing as a skeletal husk. It was the only way to make sure the world didn't go to shit. I wasn't going to make the same mistake I did with Death's Dance when I was Lissandra." I moved my jaw around to work out the hurt. Than's fury rode the bond between us. I knew he wouldn't bend with the deal I made, but it was the best thing to do. When this is over I had to find a way for him to accept this. Our love had survived lifetimes, it would survive this as well.

"What's done is done. We can deal with the ramifications later and go over this deal you struck with my brother. First, we have to go get Doni and Brenna. Follow me." Azrael was gone in a rush of wind and the gentle sound of flapping wings.

I followed behind Azrael and knew Than would come. It was in his nature to help. We arrived in a darkened temple, but there was light up ahead. The imp was beside Azrael, but when he stepped toward the light, the imp disappeared. We were in the real world and not in some limbo. Something about this place made my skin crawl. It reminded me of my house, a place where realities and dimensions intersected. That would help explain why Azrael couldn't get a read on his beloved.

Azrael stepped into the light, and I went behind him. We were surrounded by decimated stone pillars. Some were several feet high and others were a couple of inches at the base. Sand dunes towered around us. This great complex of ruins had once been a vast temple. The moon hung above us, half full. A few torches had been planted into the ground and were burning. Shadows crawled down the temple columns and stretched out along the ground. Towards the back of what I assumed used to be the altar was Brenna chained to a stone pillar. My boss was about to step foot in the sand, when I noticed a ripple in the loose grains. I grabbed his arm and gestured to the sand.

He backed away. The shadows bleeding into the sand grew larger. "How are we going to get her?" I asked.

Than grabbed a stone and threw it into the air. Once it crossed the threshold of the steps, the shadows swarmed around it until there was nothing left but a pile of ash. We couldn't fly over it. I kicked another stone into the sand. A scarab the size of a Volkswagen beetle reared out of the sand and snapped at it.

"Kerstin, is that you?" Doni's voice echoed in the night.

I strained to see her, but I didn't find her. "Doni, we'll get you out. Stay put."

"Please help me!" The pleading voice broke into hysterical laughter behind. We turned around and found Doni.

"Thank God, you're okay." I went to go toward her.

Azrael shook his head. "That's not Doni."

Her guise fell away and revealed Nephthys dressed in Doni's clothes. Why hadn't I seen it before? All along she had been hiding in plain sight. Anubis said there were others, but I hadn't thought one of his minions would be one of my friends. "You played possum and let us believe you wanted to help us. Why?"

"Someone had to lead you to Anubis. Those pathetic amateurs had no idea what they were doing. They were melting all over the place. You were a bigger fish and I took it upon myself to hook you. They were melting all over the place. I took it upon myself to hook you. Worked pretty good, too."

She was right. I'd fallen for it. "What about Hel? Was that you also?"

"No, that really was her. Once I realized she had gotten to you, I made sure to tell my son."

"How long have you been impersonating Doni?"

"For a long time now, getting a taste of life. After Tobias was killed. Anubis gave me the power and the knowledge on how to help free him. Once the door was open from your death and dealing with Mastema, it took him this long to fill the well. Then all he needed was you. It was easy to go to Doni and appear to offer my services on having an insight into death."

"What did you do to her?"

"She was meat for the sphinx. Gods she kept simpering about her life and her boyfriend who was in this coma. I tried to go after that little bird you call a psychic, but she saw it coming and had too many wards up against me. I was sure my cover would've been blown long before you brought me here."

"Let Brenna go. She has nothing to do with all of this," Azrael replied.

The goddess chuckled. "Once I felt the well break down, I knew what I had to do. You're going to pay for what you did to Anubis. Your memories were supposed to stay locked away, Anput. But no! You always had to show off with him. You always wrapped him around your little finger."

I held up my hands. "Whoa! Anubis loved me."

"And you took him away from me," she shouted. "I finally got the others to agree with me that your relationship was an abomination. Mastema was supposed to keep your memories locked away so you wouldn't come looking for him. Damn angels. Azrael put him in the box. You locked him up forever."

"You were supposed to be loyal to me. How could you disobey me? You helped me gather the other angels to my side and close him in the tomb. You were supposed to guard the entrance and alert me if someone tried to rouse him," Azrael said to her.

Nephthys laughed. "Did you think I was going to side with them? I'm not stupid. I was always going to side with him. I'm his mother. Besides, you stopped checking on any of us. You forgot about your office and what the status of it truly means. But I did what I've always planned on doing. It took this long to gather everyone and for the stars to align just right. Even if you do defeat me, there are more of us death gods on my side. Now come and get me." She faded into the shadows.

Brenna screamed. Azrael spun around and raced toward the sandpit when I caught his arm. He ripped it from me and growled flashing his fangs. The large scythe he had taken from Anubis appeared in his hand. He grew another two feet and his wings were fully extended.

"You forget who I am. She forgets who I truly am. I'm not one of the lowly death gods. I am Death. I am an Archangel, and nothing is stronger than me in this aspect. Now stay behind me."

I backed away as the coldness of his presence descended over me. The chill ran through my veins. It dulled the fire I had from Mastema's influence over me. I summoned my scythe as well and stepped behind him. Than followed me in his reaper attire. Once Azrael stepped out onto the sand, it roiled and a large scarab emerged from the ground. It tried to snatch at him. The shadows descended and tried to wrap around him. When they touched him, they shriveled and died. He swung at the scarab and split it in two. Others surrounded us, but we attacked anything that came up out of the sand. Azrael cleared the path until he reached Brenna. He yanked the chains from her wrist. Black lines spread all along her veins and marred her skin.

"Brenna," Azrael whispered.

Her eyes fluttered, but they did not open.

"Looks like you got here too late," Nephthys laughed.

Azrael raised his scythe, but I stepped before him. "Let me. I owe you at least this. Take care of Brenna," I said to my boss.

"Do you really think you can take me on? You're just a reaper."

Azrael bent over Brenna. Than fended off the occasional shadow that flew at us. The scarabs were dead. Something burned in my pocket. "I'm not just a reaper. I'm also an angel." The power of the cosmos filtered through me as did the burning power of hell. A match sparked within me. Everything I was, had been, and had become came together. I was the product of my past lives, the power Azrael granted me, and the Devil's new play thing. "You don't realize who you're talking to. I was the wife of Anubis. I have been here and back again to the other side, and you forget that. You've been standing on the edge and have forgotten what death truly is, and what you were once meant to do. You were revered, and a sister to Isis. What would she say now?"

"Who gives a fuck what she says? She's been buried under tons of sand for ages. She went to sleep when all the rest of the gods did or faded out of existence. You won't be able to take me down."

I glanced over at Azrael and a silver glow flooded Brenna's body as he held his wrist over her mouth. She breathed and latched onto his wrist. At least she's safe. At that moment, a shadow wrapped around me. Nephthys laughed. Heat ignited from my body, and I glowed in the night as flames encompassed me. The shadow screamed and burned away. I swung at Nephthys. She countered with a sickle she pulled out of nowhere. I spun out of the way, but it caught my shoulder. I hissed in pain and swung again. Each time the blades came together purple sparks dropped to the ground.

Nephthys tried to swing at me again. I reached out my arm and the threads of my robe caught her. She fell onto the ground. I held the scythe to her throat and pulled out the Eye of Horus.

"No. Get that away from me."

"Why? What does that do?" I whispered.

Azrael glanced at the eye and nodded. "It makes sure that she won't rise. You won't be meddling again. I'll see to that." Azrael waved his hand.

A sandstone coffin rose from the center of the sandpit. I placed the medallion around her neck. Nephthys screamed, but the eye paralyzed her. Azrael picked her up and placed her inside the coffin. He materialized the lid. It slid into place and sunk into the sand until it disappeared along with her screams.

"We should go," Than said.

I glanced in the direction he pointed at. Lights from approaching cars were coming. Someone noticed us. I hadn't realized there was civilization nearby. I heard the rumble of engines. I glanced over to Brenna. Some of her color had returned. "You're right. Let's go."

Azrael held Brenna to him and disappeared into a dark slit in the universe. I didn't bother with the theatrics and followed behind him. We reappeared back at his house. I picked up Angela and held her. I had been her mentor and her death was on my hands. Again, the choices we make. *I'm so sorry. I never meant for this to happen to you. I hoped I could protect you. It would have been better if you never knew me.*

"We need to talk." The muscles in Azrael's jaw clenched.

"I know, boss. But I should get her home and think of something to tell her mother," I responded.

"Let me take her." Than took her from my arms. His eyes held all the compassion for Angela and none for me.

"Thank you," I said.

He flew off before I could say anything else. Brenna walked into the kitchen. "What were you thinking when you made a deal with Mastema? I told you I was going to get out." His voice rose from a whisper to him near shouting.

"And had you?" I snapped.

He didn't answer, so I figured that was a no. "When I first saw Anubis, I was going to kill him. Then he touched me. When he shoved me into the well it unlocked all these memories. I remembered who I'd been. Anubis must have realized it. When I told him I couldn't be with him, he lost it. The power of the well had me. If I went back in there it'd be agony, but I wanted to. Then Mastema came and showed me the future."

"A possible future."

"No. The real future if I gave up. My guides confirmed it. You were dead. Than was his pet with no soul. I couldn't see him like that. The world was going to end all because of me. I couldn't make the same mistake I did when I was Lissandra and have those deaths of all those people on my head. He offered me a way to save everyone. Everything. Including you. I knew you and Than wouldn't be happy, but there was no other decision. I wasn't going to let the world burn."

"What was the contract you signed? Did you give him your soul?"

"No contract. I didn't give him my soul. My blood never touched any parchment. He gave me access to hell and made me his grim reaper. I have to harvest the souls he wants collected no questions asked. He'll allow me to keep the life I have, that you've given me. I didn't know what else to do. Would you rather I jumped into the well?"

Azrael ran his fingers through his hair and paced. A thin layer of frost laced the floor where he walked. The temperature in the room dropped ten degrees. I was screwed. I knew the moment that I said yes. *I'm probably going to be cast into some dark pit or locked away for eternity.* I sank into the nearest chair I could find. I held my head in my hands. Everything I had done was supposed to be for the good of everyone else. I needed to save them and not me. Now Doni and Angela were dead. Than would never forgive me.

"Kerstin, look at me." Azrael's flat tone only made me hate the idea more, but I looked at him anyway.

He took my hand in his. "I understand the choice you made. To be honest I couldn't have gotten out of those chains. I hate to admit that. I know you did what you thought was right, and I guess in some way it was. I believe you. Let me see." He held my face between his hands and stared into my eyes. Tears rolled down my cheeks from the intensity of reliving it and seeing Anubis again as more memories from that life rolled through my mind. Azrael wiped the tears away before taking my hands once more.

"I saw what you dealt with. I just wish there could've been another way for you."

"Are you going to banish me now?"

"No. I'm not going to banish you. I'm not going to strip you of your power or of the life you live. But I can't smooth it over with Than. He didn't take it as well. You're still one of my reapers. I can't take that away from you. And yet I can't condone the deal you made with my brother. However, there is one thing I will do."

"What's that?"

He touched my cheek. "If you need my help, I won't be there to answer. I won't cut you off from the graveyard. The other reapers will know what you've done—the good and the bad—in every realm. You can still bring souls to the cemetery. I can understand you might not want that, but I have to protect my other reapers. Do you understand?"

"I do. Can I ask you for one favor please?"

"You're pushing it."

"Please don't take this out on Than. He didn't have anything to do with it. I couldn't leave him...I—" Emotion choked me up. Than was all that mattered and now he hated me.

"Shh...shh. I'm not going to take this out on him. You should go now."

I stood up. "Okay. I'm going to say good-bye to Brenna. I'm glad she's okay."

Brenna sat at the kitchen table with a cup of tea in her hands. "I wanted to check to see how you were and apologize for bringing this trouble on you."

She waved her hand. "You did what you thought was right in both situations. I heard what you said to Azrael. Mastema's always been a persuasive bastard. I know. I had to dance with him."

"Yeah, but you said no."

She shrugged. "It was a different situation and time. Things were more complicated. It's hard to explain. It was a long time ago. Look, don't worry about Azrael. If you need anything, come to me. We can figure this out together. Just don't raise any demons or anything."

"Mastema said I was something different because of all that had been done to me. He said something about the power in me. Do you know what he was talking about?"

Her brow furrowed, and she set her cup down. Brenna took my hand and closed her eyes. Her grip grew painful. I don't know what it was that she saw, but when she opened her eyes they were haunted. "Oh, Kerstin."

"What is it? What did you see?"

Her gaze flicked to something behind me. Azrael stood in the doorway. He shook his head. Something passed between them. "I'm sorry. It's something you have to live through. Part of the path you've chosen. Remember what I said. I'm here if you need me."

"Thank you." It was time to go.

My wings carried me away.

CHAPTER FOURTEEN

I reappeared in a hospital outside an empty nurse's station. I slipped inside a room and saw Nick sitting up in the bed. He was no longer connected to the breathing tube. All the other major IV's were gone. A terrified look came over his face.

"No. I'm not ready. Don't take me. Go away."

I stared at my hands and realized I was in grim reaper attire. I banished the robe and the skull appearance. "Whoa Nick! It's me. It's Kerstin."

"Kerstin, where's Doni?" Nick asked.

How was I going to tell him that I had gotten her killed? "I don't know where she is." That was the truth. "I wanted to check in on you and make sure you were okay. What's the last thing you remember?"

His hair was completely white. The lines deepened around his eyes. He appeared ten years older than the first time I met him only a couple of years ago when Jackson dragged me to Death's Dance. "We were at the hotel, getting ready to look at the footage we caught at the reinvestigation of Death's Dance. I heard something on the audio and then…then there was this flash of light. Sometimes just flashes of pain. I couldn't stand it. Then it was gone. I don't know where I was. Where am I?"

"You're in a hospital. We went up to your room to look over the computers as you had wanted. Doni was in hysterics that you had a stroke or something. They took you away. You've been here ever since. Than and I took care of the problem, and now you're back. I wanted to make sure you were okay. Now you are, I'm going to head home. I'll send Than over to say hello." I pecked him on the cheek.

His soul was weak and reorienting with his body. I laid my hand over his heart and helped to settle him back into his body. He drew in a long breath. I felt the pain that radiated through him. I couldn't heal him, but I didn't sense anything inside of him. My senses told me he had a long while before he was supposed to be taken to the other side.

"I'm scared. What should I do if another reaper comes for me?"

"You shouldn't be frightened of them or me. If one does come you can always ask for me in the end."

"Something's different about you. I can't place it."

"Things've changed in the last few months."

"I can tell. You've gotten…I don't know. Otherworldly. I thought psychics didn't get advice about themselves."

I perched on the edge of the bed. His words rang something in my mind. "We don't. We get information about others." I squeezed his hand. "Rest. I wanted to be sure you were awake and okay. If I see Doni, I'll let her know that you're awake."

"Thank you. It's good to see you." His words pinged in my mind. What he said made me realize something. I had somewhere else to go. I didn't bother to hide my disappearance and went to my next destination.

I found myself outside of a small house with a psychic sign on the door that said closed. I glanced behind me when I realized I was by the ocean. The smell of the sea was pungent enough that it had to be low tide. I knocked on the door. It took a moment for someone to come and answer the door. Sparrow stood on the other side with red swollen eyes.

"Did I interrupt something?"

"No. A romantic comedy that turned out to be a tragedy, that and I'm getting over a cold. Come on in. I wasn't expecting you so soon."

I stepped inside. A cool rush of energy washed over me. The inside of her house was not what I expected. I did see the altar she had set up to Anubis with a black mirror and a goblet next to it with some burned out incense cones. The power from the altar blasted me. "I take it you figured out I was coming."

She shut the television off and fell back into the couch. Sparrow patted the seat next to her. "After two jackals and a goddess came to my door trying to kill me, then yeah I figured you'd be coming soon."

"At least you were able to save yourself. If I had any warning Nephthys was going after you, I would've told you and the others. Doni and Angela are dead. I couldn't save them." I collapsed on the couch. I set my head in my hands. Sparrow laid a hand on my shoulder and then pulled it away.

"Ouch! Damn you're burning up. What did you do? Why are flames surrounding you?"

"That's what I wanted to talk to you about. I thought you might have an answer or at least maybe help me figure out a way out of the predicament I've gotten myself into."

"What happened? Even I can't see what you got yourself into."

I told her everything. The details spilled out of me as I was glad to share my experience with someone who wouldn't judge me. Sparrow stopped me and offered me a bowl of ice cream. The chocolate chip helped to ease my breaking heart for the moment. Finally, the ice cream was consumed, and I was sobbing again at the idea of not being able to reconcile with Than. I wasn't worried about being shunned as a grim reaper. I was pretty much used to being alone. I set the bowl down on the table.

"Any ideas?"

She pulled her hair out of her ponytail and shrugged. "I-I-I don't know. I'm a necromancer, not one who can look into the flames of hell. How can you break a contract with the devil? That's a tall order."

"I know. I'd owe you several favors. If you can find a way it would mean...I don't think there are words for what it would mean. I can't offer you souls or anything, not that I exactly know what a necromancer does. Than told me to be careful of you, but I've always thought that we were friends. We understood one another more than many others because we have the same types of abilities. Sorry, I'm rambling."

Sparrow grabbed my hand. "Things will blow over between you and Than, but you have to go through a bit of a crazy time before they do. Just don't lose your way no matter what path you might be shoved upon. Just remember you're who you are and reconnecting with your other self is probably a good thing in the end."

"Thanks. I think. I take it that's the message you've gotten from your guides."

"Yeah."

"Don't you love how they are never straight forward?"

She snorted. "Yeah. It's wonderful. Are you going to write a book about all of this?"

"Book? How could you even think about that when I'm dealing with this crisis?"

"Sorry. It might be the ice cream or the really bad movie talking, but you should think about it when the time is right. You could have another bestseller on your hands."

I stood up and knew there was one more thing that I had to do. "Thanks, Sparrow. I'll keep that in mind. Can I ask you something first before I go?"

"Anything, Kerstin. We're friends."

"Did you have a hand in any of this with Mastema, or the serial killer at the convention, or with Anubis?"

Her expression remained neutral. "I might be a necromancer, but I wouldn't be involved with anything to do with Anubis."

"Then what's the altar for?"

"That! Oh, the mask was a gift. I don't worship Anubis. Nor was I involved in anything to do with the devil. The main goddess I pray to is Hekate. She's the one that I work with. She was the one who warned me about Nephthys coming."

"Glad that you have someone to talk to."

"You should try and find her. She's one of the more active gods. Being associated with death I thought you'd already be talking to her."

"I'll have to look her up. Thank you."

She grabbed my arm. "Doni was the one who called to Anubis. She started it all. That was how Nephthys was able to get to her."

"Why didn't you tell me this before at the convention?"

"Because by the time I figured it out, the jackals were at my door. She showed up as Doni and melted into Nephthys before me. Sometimes I'm even blind to all things. She was hiding in plain sight. Sorry. We might be both good psychics, but we don't have all the answers until they're upon us. I'm sorry."

"It's fine. I should go."

"See you around." I gave her one last smile and walked out of her house. Maybe I could contact this other goddess. Right now, I just needed to talk to Than, and I dreaded that. I thought about home and flew there quickly, glad that the familiar energy of the nexus was around me. I arrived at the graveyard and found the spirits milling about. Sarah was by her stone, guarding over it.

"You're back," she said.

"Yeah. I'm back. Have you seen Than?"

"He's in the house. I'm not sure you want to go in there."

"I don't have a choice. I'm the one he's mad at. I'd stay clear for a while. Tell the others."

She nodded.

I waved to her and walked onto the porch. The whole place was dark. The kitchen was turned upside down. The table was broken into pieces. The chairs were nothing more than kindling. There was a large dent in the refrigerator door the shape of a fist. Food was scattered on the floor. Glass crunched under my feet. A small breeze blew through the shattered windows. In the living room, all the furniture was tossed about. The photos of us lay in shreds. As I ran my fingers over a bookshelf, the images from my alter ego flashed in my mind. In her reality nothing was wrong with her house. Sparrow said to reconnect with my other self, but I didn't really know what that meant. Besides it wasn't time for that. I had to see Than. I followed the path of destruction upstairs and to our bedroom. It was darker there than the rest of the house, colder too. The shadows didn't want to reveal their secrets, but he concealed himself within them.

"Than."

"You should leave," he whispered.

"I came back so we could talk."

"There's nothing to talk about. You made your decision."

"I didn't have a choice. You know that. I couldn't leave you in that cell to rot. I couldn't leave you hurting like that. You stood by me all those lifetimes, watching out for me. You loved me through all of it. Can't you see me through this? I need you." I could barely speak after thinking about all the things that I saw while I was in that dungeon. Of seeing the thing he had become when Anubis drained all the vitality from him. I went to feel for the necklace around my neck with his feather, but then I remembered Azrael had disposed of it because it connected me to him.

"You don't know what I went through."

"I know about the scarabs."

"How?"

"They went from you and into me. I experienced what you did. Maybe not to the extent, but I did. I swear to you that I didn't have a choice." I stepped into the room and sensed he was by the window. I placed my hand on his arm and rested my head against his back. I inhaled the jasmine about him along with the masculine scent of him. I needed to feel his arms around me and know I was home, but he was so far away.

"I didn't realize," he said flatly.

"Anubis reached along our connection from the feather you gave me. Azrael had to destroy it."

"I suppose you want another one."

"I just want to know you don't hate me for what I did. I can't lose you. Azrael's already shunned me from the other reapers so I don't contaminate them."

"Do you want him? Mastema? Do you want to fuck him?"

He turned around and lifted my chin up, so I could look

into his dark eyes. I could see him now as he emerged from the shadows. His wings were folded back. His expression was dark and shadowed. I shook my head. "It's not like that. I don't want to sleep with him. He kissed me because he knew it would stir you up."

"Well, it did. But I can't condone you being his slave or whatever it is you are going to be to him." He extended a wing and plucked out one of his feathers and placed it in my hand. It shrunk down so it was the size of the pendent about two inches long. This time it was black, but I could still hang it from a chain if I wanted.

"Thank you."

Than reached around his neck and pulled off the necklace he had with my feather on it and dropped it into my hand too. "You'll need this. I don't want it anymore."

"Than, please."

"No, Kerstin. Things have changed. I know why you made the deal with Mastema. I understand it logically. The world would have been decimated by Anubis. I was imprisoned. Azrael was being tortured. I can even accept you shared a past life with him. But it feels like you betrayed me. You chose him over me. That's what my heart tells me. The heart you gave me. The soul you awakened within me has been betrayed. I— I just can't."

"But I love you."

His dark laughter filled the room. "I'm not sure I know what that is anymore. Or if you do for that matter. I'm sorry. It's over. I never thought I'd say that. Azrael was right to keep you from the others. I never thought I'd see the day where you'd become Lucifer's puppet."

"It's not like that." I clutched the feathers in my hand. "Please don't do this."

"You never told me you were connected to Anubis."

"I didn't know it until he threw me in the well, and it all came back to me. It's almost like what Azrael said, sometimes you can't win over fate. Maybe this was all supposed to happen. I don't know. But I know I need you in my life. I can't do this without you. Please."

"I'm sorry, Kerstin. I've said my peace. You and I are not the same people we were all those years ago. You're not Lissandra. Part of her still lives within you. No matter if you remember all of your past lives. She never would've accepted the devil's proposal."

"You're right. She never would have. And as Anput I never would've fallen in love with you. We all change, Thanatos. That's what happens when you have a soul. You grow. If you had seen what I saw, you would understand my decision."

He shrugged. "Maybe. But I don't know you now, and I'm not sure I can. Goodbye." Than backed away until he blended with the shadows and was no more.

Something inside of me splintered when he left. I sank onto the bed as sobs overtook me. After everything I went through, the one thing I needed the most had gone. Sparrow said we might work it out. Sometimes even the advice of the best psychics in the world didn't amount to anything. I curled up. Mind numbing grief overtook me. I descended into a darkness that swallowed me up. It was so dark that not even the strongest light could penetrate it.

****

I don't know how long it was that I lingered in the darkness of my mind. It could have been weeks or months, but when I did emerge it was only from a voice that I recognized. The first time he called to me, I didn't want to answer. But then I felt him there doing nothing except talking to me. He provided me with a light. It was dim at first and hurt my eyes, but I adjusted to it. He slowly brightened it so I could find the path back. It was slow going, fighting off the monsters that tried to grapple me and pull me back under. However, the longer I saw the light, the more I wanted to dig myself out of the dark pit I had descended into.

Each step closer brought back memories I had tried to push away. Soon his voice was the only thing that I wanted to listen to, and the darkness was something I could leave behind. And when I opened my eyes, it was to his peaceful smile and his calm green eyes. It took me a moment to focus on his round face, and the eyes that were covered with glasses.

"Welcome back," he greeted me. His voice was calming, and it forced me to concentrate on him.

"T-hank you," I whispered. My voice was hoarse as though I hadn't spoken in a long time. "W-where am I?"

"You're safe. That's the most important thing."

I half nodded and glanced around the room. I was sitting on a bed. The man in the lab coat sat on the bed next to me. Behind him were two other larger men in white uniforms with badges clipped onto their pockets. The walls were painted a faint lime green with brown stains on the walls and an enormous black patch that spread out along the ceiling tiles. The window had a large wire screen across it so I couldn't get to the glass. I glanced down at my hands and saw I was in some kind of a straight jacket. I tried to move again, and the overpowering urge to escape came over me. The orderlies rushed forward, but the man, the doctor, held up his hand to stop them.

"Kerstin, calm down. I know all of this is overwhelming to you. You are safe. You don't have to be in the dark anymore. You finally came out of the delusion that you've been in all this time."

"Delusion?" I asked him.

"Yes. But we can talk about that later. Right now, I just want you to rest. It's good to finally talk to you."

A shadow slid across the lime green wall, passed over the orderlies, and settled into the corner. At first I thought it might be the sun creeping across the sky, but it began to take form. It grew taller and took on the shape of a large man nearly seven feet tall. He leaned back against the wall. I couldn't make out much detail except that his eyes were orange and glowed like coals from the fire.

"Oh God!" I whispered.

"What is it?" the doctor asked.

"Can't you see him?" I tried to back against the wall, into the corner of my room, but I didn't have the strength. My gaze locked with the being there. The doctor looked into the corner.

"I don't see anything."

"But he's right there! Demon!" I screamed.

The shadow lifted a finger to his lips in a shushing motion and spread his dark wings until they covered the room.

"Help me with her," the doctor ordered.

I tried to get away, but the orderlies pinned me down. The shadows of his wings touched me, and I heard him whisper something in my ear, but I couldn't make it out. A needle was thrust into my arm. The next thing I knew darkness enveloped me, and I followed wherever the drugs would lead me away from the monster.

CHAPTER FIFTEEN

Six months later...

Shrieks split my head no matter how much I pressed my palms over my ears. I tried to force them away, but nothing worked. I stared into the heavy darkness but those who screamed had no faces. Dark shapes loomed over me. Their fingers dug into my flesh, burning it away. I cried out, but no one heard me. No one was there.

"Kerstin." Someone shook me awake.

I opened my eyes and looked at the man. He seemed vaguely familiar.

"Who are you?" I glanced around the room. A wire screen covered the window. Pale mint green walls surrounded me. The beige tiled floor had seen better days. Water stained blobs on the ceiling leered at me. Some twisted into skulls and others yelled. *None of this is happening. I know what's real and what's not.*

"Kerstin." The doctor touched my arm lightly. It was something recognized. He gestured for me to remove my hands from my ears.

"Yes." The subtle yells of the damned vied for my attention.

"You hear the shrieks today?"

I nodded. Wasn't it obvious?

"Are they as loud as they have been?" His pen was poised over the clipboard he had.

"They aren't so loud today, Dr. Tanner."

He jotted something down on his pad. "Good. That's very good. Can you tell me if he's here today?"

A quake of terror started in my middle toe, working its way up my foot until I tapped the arch of my foot against the metal rail at the bottom of my bed. My pulse raced. He haunted my nightmares. Beautiful. Deadly. A creature not of this world. I waited for him to rip through the thick concrete walls with demands I couldn't fulfill. "No. He's not here."

"Good. Five days in a row. It seems the treatment's working. What do you think?"

I shrugged. "Maybe."

He pulled his chair closer to the bed. "Tell me again how this all started for you. I want to be sure I have it right."

He asked me numerous times in the eight weeks since I arrived. "It all started a couple of years ago at the reunion show for Spirit Seekers. We were doing a tribute to Jackson, Sandra, and all the others who died in the tragedy from the first filming at Death's Dance. It was a miracle that me and Nick survived."

Dr. Tanner flipped a few pages back on his pad. "Why do you say miracle now when all other retellings you've said you felt you were chosen to live?"

I pulled my legs up to my chest and rested my chin on the top of my knees. The whole world had witnessed some great spectacle when it was filmed at the ghost town. "Well, it was, if you think about it. All the others died, slayed by some otherworldly force. As you said, it was captured on film. Even if people say it was faked, some things can't be explained away. That's why I say it is a miracle."

"Yes. I can see why you'd think this. I've watched this show. Whether or not they use special effects, it's clear you were afflicted by something. Events happened to you that changed how you see the world. Although, how you perceive the world is a little bit different than the average person. You say you can see and talk to spirits. As well as foretell the future."

A small giggle escaped my lips. "I *perceive* the world the way I've lived in it, and that does include wandering souls." Energy from my guides filled me. They remained a constant through this whole ordeal. The bed springs creaked as I leaned forward. "Are you wandering, Dr. Tanner?"

His pen stopped a few centimeters from his note pad. The color drained from his face. "Ms. Palmer, this isn't about me. We're talking about what brought you here in the first place."

A host of images crested in my mind. The good doctor pouring over his books late at night with one too many bottles of Jack Daniels. Him on top of a patient he counseled in his private practice. She was barely out of her teens suffering from some kind of sleep disorder. "True, but how would Cinnamon feel when you informed her you were tired of wandering down the path of her dreams? What would, Juliet, your dear wife, say if you admitted to her about your patient relationships? She already knows about it. Darling little spice girl left behind a very incriminating vibrator you like to use on her."

"Ms. Palmer, I don't know where you get your information from, but I can assure you that..."

Power crested inside of me turning me hot and cold. It was too much energy for one person to handle. The disorientation of sharing my body with another me hit me. The heaviness that something or someone combined with my spirit took on a sense of deja-vu. My existence expanded almost as though there was more of me when there shouldn't have been. It started after the reunion episode at Death's Dance. *Maybe it's another sign I'm losing my mind.* As the heat increased so did the screams of the lost. When this other energy came over me, a deep sense of loss and anger rolled through me. In these strange moments, I learned to use the borrowed power. I pushed along the lines of my doctor's life. "...that no one should know those details and yet I do."

I slipped off the bed. The tiles were cold on the bottoms of my feet, but they felt good with the warmth coursing through me. He remained stuck to his chair. His eyes didn't leave me. The notepad and pen clattered to the floor. I straddled him. His breath came in short pants. He was in dire need of a breath mint.

"Y-you really shouldn't be doing this," he stammered. The flutter of his pulse caught my eye.

"Why not? You enjoy it when your spice girl does it to you." A greater degree of heat penetrated me. A tickle of sweat slipped down my forehead. The power propelled my consciousness along the line of the good doctor's future. "She has dreams of you divorcing your wife and leaving your brat of a daughter behind," I whispered in his ear.

"H-how do you know all this?"

"Just goes along with my perception of the universe. Do you think I'm crazy now?"

"I never said you were crazy, Ms. Palmer. Just that you're certainly afflicted by something."

"If I wasn't cuckoo for Coco Puffs, then why am I in this place?"

He took a hard swallow as I trailed my fingers down his

chest. "Ms. P-palmer, you really should..."

"...continue doing that," he purred.

Before me was no longer the doctor, but the demon, the man who chased me even behind these thick walls. I tried to back off him, but he caught me around the waist. He pressed a finger to my mouth before I could scream. Terror surrounded my soul. The warmth in me fled. All I could do was stare into this beautiful, damning visage of a man. This was the closest he'd come to me in all my fevered states.

"You're not real," I whispered against his finger. The point of his black nail pressed into the dimple above my top lip.

"Of course I am, Kerstin. More real than you've ever imagined. You're mine in all ways, shapes, and forms no matter where you reside. No matter where you go."

"I'm not yours. I've never made a pact with you. Never."

He removed his finger. His golden hair spilled over his shoulders, slightly longer than it had been before. Red, orange, and black highlights caught the light in the room. His eyes were dark orange. He waited for me to give in to break my spirit. My tormentor stopped within centimeters from my mouth. He traced my lips with his finger. The sulfur from his flesh stuck to the tip of my tongue. He rested his hands on my cheeks. His skin scorched mine, but I could not pull away.

"What if I told you that you already did?"

"I wouldn't believe you."

"Stubborn, even when you're locked in here. You can't run from me forever. Hear me, Kerstin."

"What are you talking about?" The pain from his touch burned deeper into my flesh. I bit my lip to keep from crying out.

"Reach out along that connection you have and tell your other half, no more hiding. She owes me. If she doesn't answer my next call then I'll make sure you do. The winged fool who believes he's disowned you will hear your suffering. Is that clear?"

"Yes."

He patted my cheeks and the pain disappeared. "Good girl. I knew one of you would be more understanding. You really should check yourself out of here. You're not crazy."

"Then why are you here? Why do I hear the screams of the damned?"

"Those are things you need to ask yourself. Don't you think…"

"…it'd be a good idea to step away from me now?"

I blinked.

Dr. Tanner returned and the devilish man disappeared. I glanced behind me. Two orderlies waited for me to hurt the doctor. One of them had a needle in his hand. I moved off him and Dr. Tanner gestured to the orderlies to back off.

"I-I'm sorry," I sputtered as the tears plopped down my cheeks. I retreated to the bed and curled up against the wall. Dr. Tanner whispered something to the orderlies. The cold and heat left my body, but the words of the hallucination threaded through my thoughts. I trailed my tongue over my lips and tasted the sulfur. *He was here. He's real. I'm not crazy.*

"It's okay. I take it you thought you were having a conversation with him?" Dr. Tanner scribbled something on his pad.

"Yes. He was where you were. I couldn't help myself. It was like I was overcome with w-wantonness."

He got up and turned my face left and right. "The important thing is that you didn't act on this sensation of lustfulness. Can you tell me where you got these?" He traced something on my cheeks.

"Got what?"

He lifted his metal clipboard so I could see my reflection. Red hand impressions as if someone burned me adorned my skin. "I don't know where I got them."

"Hmm…They're bigger than your hands. Maybe they're psychosomatic. You've never exhibited any of these symptoms before."

"There's another one there." I pointed to the end of the bed. A handprint was burned into the sheets showing the neatly charred edges on the yellowed fabric. I placed my hand over the mark to show it was bigger than my hand. Dr. Tanner did the same. It was also bigger than his hand as well.

"Isn't that strange? I wonder how you did that."

"Me." *How could he think I did that?* "I didn't do that. You were watching me the whole time?"

"There are ways. We're going to have to take a different turn in our therapy."

My stomach twisted at the comment. "I don't think so."

Dr. Tanner flashed me a small smile. "Isn't that why you're here? To make yourself better."

"I think I want to check myself out."

"That's your prerogative. Why don't you take the night and think on it?" Dr. Tanner got up from the bed and walked out of the door. "I'm sure you'll come to the right conclusion once you wake up in the morning."

He slammed the door shut leaving me to think about all that happened. I trailed my finger over the burnt sheet and closed my eyes trying to convince myself it was a vivid hallucination. No matter how I tried to rationalize it away, I knew it was all real.

I wasn't crazy after all.

CHAPTER SIXTEEN

I rubbed my eyes and pushed the sleep away. Odd dreams targeted me when I slept. Sleep used to be my solace, but now it was only another place where Mastema could find me. I was exhausted from running and hiding. Everywhere I went he found me eventually. The devil wanted me to fulfill my duty to him. He might not have owned my soul, but I was bound to him. He had a leash around me, marked me so I had the power of hell along with my reaper powers. I'd become the Devil's bitch. Being in my graveyard brought me some solace.

Whenever I was there, I sensed watchful eyes on me. The other reapers ostracized me because of my pact with Mastema to save the world from Anubis. When I thought of Anubis, the memories of the life we spent together were all like some dream. He remained in my mind like a pleasant memory, but he was behind me the same way my life as Lissandra was.

"You can't keep blaming yourself for what happened."

I glanced over at Sarah. She wasn't scared to talk to me. "I'm a pariah. Azrael's shunned me. Than won't speak to me. I'm the Devil's minion. Tell me how to stop my life from turning into an even shittier pile?"

Sarah patted my arm. "You saved the world in more ways than you know. You did what you thought was right. You weren't acting on impulse. The Lord of the Dead only does what he think's best because he doesn't want the others involved with the dark one. Than is upset because he thinks you desire to sleep with the fallen one."

"Tell me something I don't know."

"You know I can't do that. I haven't been beyond the boundaries of this property since I died. I rather like it here. And I have you to talk to."

"I know."

"You need someone else to talk to."

"Who?"

"What about that other woman you spoke about? The other psychic?"

"Sparrow? The necromancer? I don't want to expose her to the Devil's antics."

The ghost brushed a piece of her brown calico dress and glided through a tombstone closer to the boundary of the boneyard. "Not her. The other one like you."

Brenna. She said I could talk to her if I needed to. I've been so busy running, I forgot. "Maybe."

Sarah turned back to me as she faded out. Her voice carried on the ethereal wind. "Why not give it a try? You might find what you're looking for."

Can I ever find the peace I crave? Can the hole in my heart ever be filled without Than? I clutched the feathers on the chain around my neck. One was his and the other was mine, pulled from our wings. I shed many tears over the past few months calling out to him in the darkness. Even if he did hear my calls he ignored them. *Sarah's right. I need to confide in someone.* The world swirled around me as I thought about Brenna.

It was easy to hone in on her because her energy vibrated at a higher frequency than mine did. It was like comparing a hummingbird to a grasshopper. The energy guided me across dimensions to the parallel Earth she lived on. I arrived in front of a building with the front facade under construction. People filtered in and out of the building. The noise of Boston made me flinch. A group of tourists skirted around the homeless man in the next doorway over as he panhandled for money. Across the street was one of the oldest cemeteries in the country where people walked the paved paths marveling at the dusted remains of the nation's forefathers. No souls lingered around the slate headstones. A bright silver portal lit the back of the graveyard. The gentle pull of it reached out to me.

"Brenna's upstairs, Kerstin."

I focused back on the voice next to me. A tall, thin black man leaned against the lamp post, inhaling a cigarette. Silver sprouted in his dark mustache. The dark purple aura around him identified him as another reaper, but there was also a ring of light like mine. He was psychic and still practicing. Peter helped me the last time I was here looking for Brenna.

"Thanks, Peter."

He placed a hand on my shoulder. "It's not hopeless."

Fingering the feathers, I flashed him a small smile. "Thanks. It feels that way. At least you're talking to me."

"I've never been one to play by all the rules. Just remember you might have to reconnect with yourself before things start to make sense. And even then…well just don't let the darkness get you."

I headed into the building past the security guard sitting

at the desk. He didn't see me because I didn't want him to. An illuminated directory board showed the Tearoom was on the seventh floor. I rode the elevator up and got off. Brenna sat at a table in the corner. Light poured onto the back of her dark brown hair from the window behind her giving her a halo. She didn't look up as the cards passed between her fingers. The door clicked shut behind me. She shuffled, slowly.

"You've come seeking solace," her voice remained flat. I didn't have to alter my perception to realize someone was talking through her.

"I did, but not from you. I came to speak to Brenna."

A smiled curled up the edge of her lips. "If you don't wish to hear what has to be said, then call out to the dark one. He'll willingly take your call."

"That's not funny." I pulled out the seat in front of her and sat down.

"I didn't think it was a joke."

"Say your peace so I can talk to Brenna."

"As you wish." She tapped the facedown card on the table with her fingernail and turned it over. The Devil.

Fucking figures. "Should I just call out to him now?"

"You know this is your present. You're enmeshed with the dark one. He has a hold on you that stretches to all corners of your being. Even if you run from him, he can find a part of you."

This wasn't the first time someone told me that. All my lives were connected. *All pieces of my soul are…Oh shit!* The realization hit me. When Azrael bid me to become human once more, I had been dead for two years. The only way to make sure I had somewhat of a human vibe so the devil wouldn't find me, they connected to the only other part of me. The other part of me lived in the same house I did. She hadn't died at Death's Dance.

Normally when a soul died, most of their other incarnations died as well so when they came together they could all pass on. At times our paths crossed. I glimpsed the shadow of her. Lately, I could feel her more. Sometimes it seemed we were so close that we shared the same existence. In my dreams, it seemed I was in a different place.

"Yes. You see now."

"Mas…"

"Do not say his name!" her tone commanded.

"Sorry. He's found the other side of me then."

"True. The dark one's made it a habit of visiting the slice of you that remained human. It's unraveling her."

"What can I do about it? I can't push my consciousness into hers. Why is this so important that you are telling me this?"

Brenna grabbed both my hands. "Things in the universe must be set right. You must live up to the bargain you struck with the dark one. You must realize what you are."

"Why? What balance must be offset? I played out my part in the ripples my past self caused. What more do I have to do? I stopped him from coming through into my reality. I stopped Anubis from being freed. I survived being ripped apart in the well of souls. I lost the man I loved. What more do I have to sacrifice? What more do I have to realize?" Wet trails slid down my cheeks, and I couldn't wipe them away because she still had my arms.

"Sacrifice. Yes. You've done much of that. But there are still ripples. Because of what Azrael did to you and you plunging into the well of souls it's fashioned you into something more. And then you made the deal with him. He's tried to woo you, using all his power. Because of the changes in you, he can't twist you into his minion."

"That's a blessing." A surge of strength pushed through

me, and I broke her hold. This time I grabbed her arms. "With all these changes, Oh Great One, what the hell have I become? Do you have an answer for me? What am I going to do with the human side of me? What am I going to do to convince Than? He thinks I'm going to fuck the devil, and that's what Lucifer wants. He wanted to drive a wedge between us so I'd only have him to rely on."

"Has he tempted you?"

"No. He always leaves me with a choice. I never signed my soul over to him. I just agreed to be his minion. When I went into the well of souls, it jarred lose memories of when I had lived a life with Anubis. What else is locked away in my soul? Mastema said I was something different if I only accepted it."

Brenna shook her head. "Kerstin, figure out what you want to fight for. If Mastema pushes your buttons, then push his back. I know you look at this as Azrael's punishment, but maybe you should look at it a different way."

"What way is that?"

"You're free."

"I still have to answer to Lucifer."

"Yes, you do. Right now, you're being held prisoner by what you're running from. You made an agreement with him. You said that he doesn't own your soul. He's letting you live the life you had before with hardly any consequences."

"But there are consequences. You want me to work for the devil? Reapers are neutral. We don't take sides."

She squeezed the bridge of her nose. "What exactly did he make you agree to? What were his words? Those are the true things that bind him if he makes a promise. You've done the dance of words with him as I have and you got information out of him before."

"He said he could give me protection. He would own me in body, but I cut him off because I wasn't going to be his in soul. He agreed to that. He said I'd be his grim reaper and collect souls without question. I'd still have all the things Azrael gave me. But Mastema would have access to me wherever I was. He said he would hammer out the details later."

"He said collect, not deliver, correct?"

"Yes."

Brenna flipped a card over. The World. "Everything is free and clear when it comes to him. He's working within the bargain you made. He has access to you, but it's not to you specifically that he is coming."

"No. It has to be the other slice of me."

"You mean you are not the sum of all your incarnations?" Brenna asked.

"Than had to rewrite time and space and link me to my other half. I don't know if she was ever supposed to die the same time the first time I did in Death's Dance or what happened. She lives her life as a psychic, an author, doing what I'd be doing if I didn't have the calling to take souls."

"Okay. So he's as bound to his original agreement as you are. You never 'hammered' out the details. You have to collect the souls he tells you to, but that doesn't mean you have to release them to him. I think you might have the upper hand in this. You just have to find your footing. Look, Kerstin, I know you want to be free of this deal. I'm sure there's a way around it. I can't give you that answer. I know you want Than back in your arms. Maybe the only way to do that is to see how this thing plays out. Go confront your other half. Confront Mastema. You're running out of fear. I understand, but don't run any more. Face the devil and win."

She pulled out another card, but didn't turn it right side up.

"Not going to let me see where my fate lies?"

"Who says the future's written in stone? We only read the paths clearer to us. They shift and change with each decision we make. Kerstin, you came here to get my advice more than you did to be cajoled. If you listened to your guides then you'd know this, but you've shut this off. I think it's your way to hide from him. But you need to open yourself up." She got up from the table and hugged me. Her frigid power packed a punch.

"Embrace what I've become." The words rang true. "I'm still going to wonder what's going on with Than."

Brenna touched the feathers that hung from my chain. "He's okay, you know."

I nodded, emotion clogged the words I wanted to say. I figured if something happened to him I'd feel it. He was always going to be in my heart. "Thank you."

"You can find him if you ever really need to. He can block you out, but the link between you can never be truly severed. You're part of one another. At the end of the day, he still loves you."

"That's nice to hear. I feel a little lost without him around. He's been there since I can remember."

"Maybe it's a good thing. You need to find your footing again. So does he. He's been tied to you in various lifetimes. No matter how many incarnations you go through, you'll always have a touch of death. If you'd never been drawn to Death's Dance in the first place, then you never would have reawakened that ability. Than would have been the specter in your dreams."

"But that's not what happened." I contemplated what she said. It was true. Than and I were bound together for a long time. Maybe I was still holding on to the part of me that was Lissandra and the feelings she had for Than. But my heart said no. I could understand the need for us to be apart. Sometimes it was the same advice I gave clients when it came to their significant others. Space until they could figure things out. *I've been hiding for the last six months from Mastema and from myself. Brenna's right. It has to stop. I have to embrace who I am. If not, it's going to destroy me. The same way the guilt had when I was Lissandra.*

I ran my fingers over the stack of Tarot cards. Brenna didn't object when I touched them the way some psychics did. Sometimes you didn't want another person messing with the energy of the Tarot. I separated them into three piles and tried to reach out to my guides. It'd been a long time since I called out to them. I turned my back on them, abandoning the very beings who could help me all because I was running from anything that would lead the devil back to my doorstep.

My guides welcomed me back without a bit of anger. "Thank you." I flipped over the first card. The Tower. My life being shaken at the foundations and ripped apart.

The second stack revealed The Hermit. Alone. Solitude. Someone taking time to find enlightenment or trying to find that light in the darkness. I could see some of that. Maybe my coming here was finding the insight I needed. Heeding the advice of a friend and getting out of my own way or pulling my head out of my ass. I smirked at that one. The last one. I pulled the third one and turned over the top card.

The Devil.

"Figures."

"It doesn't necessarily mean—"

"You and I both know it does."

Brenna took the card and wiggled it together until another one came off the back of it. She slipped her hand over it before I got a look at it. "Keeping secrets?"

She looked at me with the same blank expression she'd met me with earlier. "Do you know the future?"

"No. I don't know the future. But I'm going to write my own from here on out."

"Good. That's the correct answer. Time to go find yourself."

CHAPTER SEVENTEEN

Rain pounded the windows and shook the screen covering the glass. I paced the room. The other patients howled and screamed, but I could deal with those rather than the demonic shrieks I heard from the shadows. Those evaporated as the storm came on. Even the water stain on the ceiling vanished. Dr. Tanner rescheduled and looked at other treatment options for me. The idea didn't bode well. It seemed any minute something would come through that door. I prayed it wouldn't be him. He terrified me and intrigued me all at the same time. Lightning lit the sky outside. The lights flickered and went out. More people screamed. A cold chill blasted through the small space. A sense of foreboding came over me. I tried to reach out to my guides to see if they had any otherworldly advice. They remained silent.

Thunder rumbled outside. The room darkened. The sound of the rain disappeared. A shadow settled on the wall across from me. I backed up until I hit the bed and stared at the slit. Something emerged from the darkness. A large figure clad in a black cloak stood before me. Its head remained down, and its hands were covered by the sleeves on the robe. Another frigid blast came from the crack. When I looked closer, I saw blinks of light. Stars. The information hit me as the fissure sealed itself. The figure remained. It didn't feel like him.

"What are you? Are you one of his minions?"

It shook its head.

"Then what are you?"

It lifted its hood and revealed its true face.

Me.

"What kind of trick is this?"

"It's no trick," the other me answered. Even with the same tone as I had.

She could have been my twin. Every detail was exact except her eyes. Something haunted her eyes. They held a wisdom and a weight I didn't understand. "Then who are you?"

"I'm you. Well, a slice of you."

"Impossible. He sent you, didn't he?" I snarled.

The silence around us continued. Lightning illuminated the room. Where she stood, frost spread out around her feet. "Mastema didn't send me. Although, since you're referring to the devil, I know he's been visiting you. I confess that's my fault. That's what I'm here to talk to you about."

She named him for certain as the devil. *Either her being here's another part of my imagination, or this is all true. He said it's true. She's saying the same thing.* He'd left behind my burned sheet and the marks on my face even Dr. Tanner couldn't explain away. "Why is it your fault?"

"What are you doing in this dump?" The other Kerstin ran her fingers over the wire screen.

"He, the d-devil, came after me. He kept coming, and I'd hear these screams. I tried to get away from him, but he kept coming, telling me I'd have to do what he wanted eventually. That he owned me. I thought I was going crazy, so I checked myself in here. Lately, Dr. Tanner's been a little off. I don't know. I think it's time to get out of here, but they won't let me go. If I'm not crazy, then why am I talking to myself?"

She sat on the edge of the bed and raked her fingers through her hair. "What do you remember about the first investigation at Death's Dance?"

"Nothing spectacular happened until the end. The whole town was visible and solid. No one had ever seen anything like it. Jackson went on raving about having proof of death being real. He was a little crazed on the subject."

"Yeah. He could get like that. Sorry. Go on?"

I wanted to ask her how she knew about the ghost town and Jackson, but I had a feeling that would come later. "After the town was solid, even with the ghosts there, it got really quiet and cold. We recorded screams and these dark shadows darting around. The tapes show Jackson knocked me out and dragged me up to the old hanging tree. I came to, long enough to feel this pain slicing through me. Jackson was dead in my arms. The recording shows some kind of tornado or big swirl of dust around the tree. It disappeared in a blink of light along with the shadows. Jackson died of a heart attack. The pain I felt was gone. After that I wrote the book, promoted the show, and did the reunion show. Then these flashes of heat hit me. They would come and go. Then more flashes of cold and sorrow. Is that because of you?"

The other me wiped a tear from her cheek and played with something around her neck. "Yes. All of it is because of me."

"Who did you lose?" Some of the pieces started to fall into place. My fear for her fell away as I sensed her grief. I settled next to the bed and rested my hand on her leg.

"Did you ever have dreams of a cloaked figure in a

graveyard?"

"There were dreams. Sometimes I'd see a shadow lingering out of the corner of my eye, but nothing bad. I never felt evil from him. Just longing. I'm not sure. He disappeared after Death's Dance. Who is it?"

"Do you remember Jackson saying he thought he caught the personification of death on film? That's why he brought you to Death's Dance in the first place."

"Yeah. But he was also a pushy pain the ass," I said to my other half.

"He was."

"Jackson was right. In my reality, things happened very differently at Death's Dance. I died and became a grim reaper. The shadow you saw was Thanatos, Than, my soulmate. The reason the devil's bothering you is because I made a deal with him. In order to help me save the world, I became his grim reaper."

Grim reapers and soulmates? "You're talking about coming from another dimension or something."

"A parallel world actually. You were never supposed to exist. You were supposed to have died at Death's Dance, and we were supposed to be smooshed back together. Azrael, my boss, kept a small slice of my soul. Two years later, while you went on with your normal life, I reaped souls. Azrael needed me to be human again. He had Than reweave my reaper self back into the history of my reality and anchor it with that small slice that remained."

"Me?" All of this should have shocked me, but it rang true. I sent up a question about the scenario to my guides. They came back with it as being truthful.

"Yes. You were the other slice they kept alive. In your house, haven't you ever wondered why some things move? Or at times you crash into something and feel like deja-vu or something walked over your soul?"

"Yeah. Freaks me out. I've gotten used to it though."

"You're crashing into me. Our house is a nexus. It made it easier for Than to connect us. When he did, I was set back on your path. The writing, the reunion show, and everything you'd done in the last two year span."

"Why are you here now? Shouldn't there be some universal paradox if we're together?"

The storm outside raged, and the window shook again. The patients' screams sounded again. The other Kerstin looked over at the door. She got up. A scythe appeared in her hand. Her face changed to a skull, and her fingers turned to bone. I went to say something, but she placed a finger to her lips to quiet me. I got up, but she motioned for me to get behind her.

The door swung open and Dr. Tanner stood in the doorway. "Well. Well. I wasn't expecting you. Torturing her has been fun. Even if it wasn't really you."

"Dr. Tanner, what are you doing here?"

"That's not your doctor."

I looked at the other me. "Of course he is. He—"

"Oh, but she's right. Dr. Tanner was good enough to eat. He made me stronger and gave me all the information about you, Kerstin," the false doctor said.

"His name is Whiro. He's a death god who sided with Anubis and sought to free him. He's up to no good."

"You put Anubis back in his coffin. And now you're going to pay." He rushed at the other Kerstin. I jumped back as I felt her move. He rushed closer. His mouth widened as though he were a snake and he was going to swallow her whole. Blue flame lit the dark room. Fire caressed the blade. She swung her scythe and his head came off. His body crumbled to the floor in ashes.

"Why was he trying to kill you or us?"

"Long story. Come on. We can't stay here. More will come." She offered me her hand.

"What happens if I go with you?"

"We'll no longer be we. Want to stop thinking you're crazy?"

Her offer lingered between us. I wanted to not be insane. I enjoyed my life, but her life sounded more fun. I posed the silent question to my guides. They helped me through the hard decisions in my life, and they said yes in unison. I slipped my hand into hers and was whisked away.

We landed in a graveyard. Stone markers surrounded me on all sides. This place was peaceful. The grass was evenly cut. The air smelled somewhat sweet, but it was thick to breathe. No names were carved into the stones. Something about it seemed so familiar. I gripped the top of the burial stone. Flashes came at me so quickly I couldn't flesh them out. I saw people moving to a fog. Unholy beasts rampaging in this space. Heard the screams of those they attacked. Pain in my back where I was ravaged. It came as quickly as it went.

"This is an odd place."

"Think of it as a purgatory."

"Why are we here?"

"Because I need someone to put us back together."

"Who can do that?"

"Azrael."

CHAPTER EIGHTEEN

Looking at myself was a shock. Being around her felt like I was being pulled toward her. I felt the missing part of me that was her that wanted to be put back together. She was me down to every detail. And yet our lives deviated because of everything we had experienced. We both had questions, but I couldn't answer them all. I hadn't expected the other death god to be hanging out in the insane asylum either.

I listened to the comic winds for Azrael. His words echoed in my thoughts that when I called out to him he wouldn't be there. But I didn't know anyone else to call to do what had to be done. Mastema might know how to put me back together again, but I wasn't up to facing him yet. Finding my other half was easier than I thought. Once I quieted my mind and focused, accepting my Fate, I found her. She was me, but in a different reality even then from Brenna. She had taken all of it in stride. I gave her props for not running away screaming.

No answer came back from my boss.

"Azrael, you owe me this."

"How can I owe you anything? Your choice was clear." A

blast of cold air hit me. The other me gasped.

"Holy Shit."

"What is this?" Azrael asked.

"She's the small slice of me you needed to remain human so I could be the bait. She's the one Than tied me to. I need you to put us back together."

"Is this what you want?" Azrael asked the other me.

The other Kerstin sighed. Her brows furrowed, and she chewed her bottom lip. Something about her seemed so innocent. She hadn't seen or experienced the things I had. And yet she had been haunted by Mastema. Part of me wished to have that innocence back to not know what lurked in the shadows. I needed her to say yes. I needed to be whole so I could stop running.

"What happens if you do this? What happens to me?"

Azrael raked his sharpened nails through his hair. His eyes narrowed. "Your memories become hers. In some respects, you die. You'll be whole and part of whatever reality this Kerstin survives in."

"Will it stop him from coming after me? Will I be safe?"

"Yes," I answered.

My boss shot me a dangerous look. His black eyes glowed red. The curve of his fangs glinted in the dim light. "You won't even realize what's going on. But yes, Mastema won't be bothering you."

"Then yes. I want this to stop. I haven't felt right really for the last couple of years. And crashing into one another has gotten a little old," the other me replied.

"Can you give us a minute?" Azrael said to her.

"Sure."

Azrael took my arm and guided me a few steps away. "I told you not to call upon me. You've been cut off from the others.

Why are you doing this?"

"This isn't about me. All right it is about me, but not in the way you think. Mastema's been terrorizing her."

"Because you've been running from him."

"What did you expect me to do? I have no one. It doesn't matter what I did was for the good of the world. You turned your back on me. The other reapers are following your ruling and Than…" I swallowed the emotion and fought back the tears. Azrael tightened his hold on me, but I broke away from it and walked away. I needed to breathe as the familiar ache of Than's loss overtook me.

"I'm sorry, Kerstin." His words drew me from the dark precipice I found myself on when I thought about my soulmate. "I didn't know about Than. I thought maybe he'd—"

"He hasn't. Spare me the lecture once more about my choices. Can you fix this? Fix me so at least I'm whole. Then you don't have to hear from me unless the world is ending again because I screwed up."

Azrael turned me around, touched my face. "I will grant you this."

"Thank you. What do I need to do?"

"Wait here."

Azrael walked over to the other me. He said something softly to her. Before she could answer, I felt a sharp pain in my chest. I couldn't breathe and fell to my knees. Pain radiated through my entire being. I clutched my chest looking for a wound but didn't see or feel anything. It seemed all of me were dying. Azrael stood over me licking his stained crimson fingers.

"What did you do?"

He knelt beside me. The world around me grew dark as the life drained out of me. He opened his mouth and sunk his fangs into the heart in his hand. The world began to fade away.

"I reunited you the only way you could be. When you wake up, you'll be whole. Then you won't have to worry about my brother pestering the other half of you. She'll be inside of you. Know this Kerstin, I won't answer the next time you call."

I struggled to hang onto consciousness. I grabbed his hand as a small bit of heat ran through me. I didn't try and stop it as the touch of hell came into me. "Wait."

"Kerstin, I—"

I pulled the necklace from my neck and put it in his hand. "Tell Than, you took away my power. That you killed me. Anything. So he can find some peace with whatever I've done. So he can move on and find solace. Please."

He took the necklace and touched my forehead. "Sleep and wake with a clear consciousness. I'll tell him."

A frigid wave gripped my body. It calmed me and eased the hole in my heart and soul. It wove deep within my spirit. I followed it down and stopped fighting the heat. As the darkness overtook me, warmth wove together with the coldness Azrael imparted me. I didn't push it away. I had been denying my fate all this time and tearing myself apart. The only way to go anywhere was to go forward.

****

When I opened my eyes, I remained in the graveyard. I touched my chest and found there was no wound. Nothing remained of my other self. And yet, I recalled the horror as Azrael came over to me. His face was not the angelic one I was used to, but the vampire. And then the pain as he pulled my heart from my chest. I recalled the hours of conversations with Dr. Tanner and the days I spent on book tours and the shadows creeping into my bedroom. I possessed my other self's memories. I also felt her innocence, but it didn't fill the pit in my heart from missing Than. However, I knew having Azrael tell Than about my death, it would free him to live his life. I closed my eyes and thought about my guides.

"Are you still with me?"

"We're always going to be with you. No matter what decisions you make."

"Are you the same ones who helped the other me?"

"We're all you need. It doesn't matter who we are."

Their comforting presence encompassed me in a warm hug of energy. They also gave me the boost I needed. I accomplished one thing. All parts of me were complete. One thing was left to be done. Although I knew I wasn't going to Hell in order to present myself to Mastema. Instead, I walked through the graveyard and took in the serenity of it. Brenna's words filtered through my thoughts. The devil told me I was to collect his souls no questions asked. But he never said I had to deliver the souls to him. He wasn't going to appreciate that, but I didn't give a shit. He never hammered out the details of the contract. I could deal with his advances because it was my choice to fall under his spell. It was my last wish to betray any memory of the man I loved.

I walked until I got to the wall of fog that separated the dimension to the higher realms. I placed my hand on it and closed my eyes. The whispers of the spirits on the other side were obscured. The cold tug inside of me told me I was still a reaper. Azrael had given me more power when I went up against Anubis. I hadn't explored that, but the coldness had grown. Within my mind's eye, I saw the dark flame of the cold power. Entwined with it was the orange flame from the power of hell. Within its heart was something else. Another part of me. All the events made me a hybrid, and I hadn't explored that yet either. I didn't think I was brave enough to embrace it yet.

I pulled my hand away and willed myself back home. The air was still. The graveyard deserted. My house looked disjointed like the pieces of a puzzle that hadn't come together right. All were the different realities coming together and clashing. When I blinked, the pieces shifted. Bright orange lit one of the cracks in the nexus. The portal to hell that Mastema came through. It was obvious as to why he could never come through fully.

My heart fluttered as I thought about what I was going to do. Hiding was no longer an option. I felt for my necklace for comfort, but recalled I'd given it to Azrael. It was gone now. My life was gone and I was the devil's servant.

"Mastema."

His name left my lips. I expected the ground to shake and the sky to rain down fireballs. None of that happened. Instead the world around me froze. The pieces in the nexus stopped. The one portal to hell yawned open like a great mouth getting ready to swallow my house. For a second I glimpsed a dark red flash exit the doorway before it sunk back in on itself and the pieces resumed moving.

"It's something isn't it?"

He stood next to me, but I didn't bother to look over. "It is."

"Have you ever seen it this clearly before?"

"No. I've just felt the universes clashing together."

"You're whole. That might have something to do with it."

"Probably. What does it matter? I'm here, ready and reporting for duty."

"Kerstin." He touched my arm. His voice wasn't seductive just ordinary.

I glanced over at him. Mastema's luster remained, the

beautiful angel, but his touch didn't rouse any feelings of lust. He stood before me nothing more than an ordinary man would. "I'm not here for chit chat. We made a deal. You helped free me from the well and released Azrael. Here I am." I stared into his eyes and didn't look away. Whatever thrall he had over me before seemed to have fallen away.

"I'm not going to be a slave driver. I know you've suffered a lot. I sympathize with you. If you let me, I can take away all that pain." He ran his finger down my cheek.

"I'm not interested in having my pain taken away. It's all I have now. Along with my memories. You're my boss until I can figure a way to get out from under your thumb."

"You can try, but I don't ever plan on letting you go," Mastema smirked.

"Maybe not, but I'm not going to be yours forever."

"We'll see. We'll see."

"What do you want me to do?"

The devil shrugged. "Nothing for now. You'll know when I want you to fetch a soul."

"So I just live my life until you call?"

"That was part of our agreement. You keep the life Azrael granted you. Stay part human. Do your book tours and write. Shuttle souls to the side when the need arises. I don't need you right now. All I wanted was for you to acknowledge you were mine."

"I've done that. No go away and leave me alone."

He trailed his thumb over my lower lip. "I could stay and make it more interesting."

"I'm not interested. Please leave."

A look of confusion passed over him. Mastema's power flashed through me, but my own power countered it. Something within me stirred. The meshed flame I saw earlier flared. It burned bright behind my eyes and filled me with an electric blue flame that bordered on white, the hottest part of the fire. Whatever I'd become had awakened with his power surging through me. I grabbed his wrist and slapped it away from me.

"There you are," he whispered. Mastema walked around me, taking in my new energy.

My wings flared out. Instead of being black as they were before, they had changed color. Silver feathers replaced some of the black ones. He reached for one of my wings. I hissed and pulled them back. He backed away and held up his hands.

"Forgive me."

"You don't touch me without my permission." I stepped toward him. He stepped back. The power rose out of me. Whatever it was, it rivaled his. I didn't understand it, but I saw fear in his eyes.

"I'm sorry, Kerstin. It won't happen again. Can you tone down the light please?" He had his hand up to cover his eyes.

I looked at my hands. The glow around them was brighter than I'd seen before. I could feel the strength surging through me, a mixture of hot and cold. Death and Hell. But there was also my human side. My heart continued to beat. My soul remained. I pulled back the power and saw the flame dim within my mind. He put his hand down and flashed me an uneasy smile.

"What am I?"

"Unique. I don't know what you are. Something that's never been before. A creation brought upon by unusual circumstances. Azrael has no idea what he has on his hands. But I'm sure he'll figure it out soon enough when you start burning shit up."

"Just go."

He flashed me his remarkable smile and disappeared. Once

he was gone, I breathed a sigh of relief. I had done it. I stood up to Mastema. He had awakened something in me, I didn't feel any different. I sighed and walked back to the house. Sarah stood at the perimeter of the graveyard and waved before she faded away. Calm returned to me, and I went inside the house. It felt the same as it did before.

Yet it was still as empty.

A wave of exhaustion filled me. I closed the door and locked up. My body felt as drained as my spirit. I crawled into an empty bed and let sleep carry me away.

CHAPTER NINETEEN

Instead of sinking into sleep, I found myself lodged into a dream. I stood atop a knoll under a skeletal tree that spread its shadow over the land below me. Frayed ropes swung from the branches. Old bones littered the ground. A skull stared at me as it lay on a large root. The old hanging tree watched over Death's Dance. It was one of the first places I was brought to where I met Than. I glanced around, but his familiar shadow didn't fall anywhere.

Why am I here? Even in this dream state, I was back at the place where it all started. The ghost town was as much a nexus as my house was. Even more so, the wound suffered here couldn't be closed because of all the souls taken. All of the lives taken. I looked down and saw the old ghost town waver in and out like a flickering film. A breeze stirred the air. I heard a faint tinkling sound.

I followed it around the tree and saw something swinging from one of the branches. As I got closer, I realized what it was. My necklace with both feathers attached to it. I took them and found they were real. "What are you doing here?" I placed it around my neck. I knew it would come back with me out of the dream.

A branch breaking made me jump. I looked back to the tree trunk and saw a dark shadow leaning against it. I dared not imagine who it was or if he was a figment of my imagination.

"Hello."

"Hello."

"What are you doing here?"

The weight of Than's gaze settled on me. My pulse echoed in my ears as he took a while to respond. "Azrael said you were dead."

"In some ways I am."

"I had to see for myself. I saw you call upon him. And then you changed. You're you and something else."

"I'm still me."

"You are."

"Why bring me here?"

"It all started here."

"It did."

"I figured it might need to end here, too."

My heart fell. "I understand. It's good to see you though. I'm glad you're okay."

"Are you that ready to have it end?"

"I don't understand. You just said."

"I said it has to end here. But I think it can also begin here. Again."

"I'd like that."

He extended his hand. "I'm Thanatos. People call me Than."

"Kerstin," I shook his hand. "It's nice to meet you, Than."

He flashed me his usual smile. My heart filled again. If this was the start of something new, then the future wasn't written.

Brenna had hidden the final outcome of her reading from me. Maybe she knew this all along. Fate had given me a new chance. It made me into something new while letting me keep the things that made the old me. Now it was giving me another chance to get to know the man I loved.

I remained a grim reaper.

I'd always be an angel.

The devil was my boss now.

The energy of the cosmos called out to me.

I could tell the future.

I can take a soul.

But mine was already bound to another.

I had done horrors in the past.

I had made the wrong choices.

My future wasn't written in stone. For once I knew, with all certainty, whatever lay before me would be great, and I wouldn't have to face it alone.

ABOUT THE AUTHOR

Crymsyn Hart is a national bestselling author of over seventy paranormal romance and horror novels. Her experiences as a psychic have given her a lot of material to use in her books. She currently resides in Charlotte, NC with her hubby and her two dogs. If she's not writing, she's curled up with the dogs watching a good horror movie or off with friends.

To find out more about Crymsyn Hart, please visit her website at www.crymsynhart.com

www.ingramcontent.com/pod-product-compliance
Lightning Source LLC
Chambersburg PA
CBHW020832260626
47169CB00003B/946